THE PRICE OF
RETRIBUTION

THE PRICE OF RETRIBUTION

BY

SARA CRAVEN

First published in Great Britain 2012
by Mills & Boon, an imprint of Harlequin (UK) Limited.
Large Print edition 2013
Harlequin (UK) Limited, Eton House,
18-24 Paradise Road, Richmond, Surrey TW9 1SR

© Sara Craven 2012

ISBN: 978 0 263 23154 0

Harlequin (UK) policy is to use papers that are natural,
renewable and recyclable products and made from
wood grown in sustainable forests. The logging and
manufacturing process conform to the legal environmental
regulations of the country of origin.

Printed and bound in Great Britain
by CPI Antony Rowe, Chippenham, Wiltshire

PROLOGUE

July

THIS flat was smaller than his previous one, yet now it seemed strangely vast in its emptiness, an echoing space, rejecting him as if he was an intruder.

He stood in the doorway of the sitting room, his gaze moving restlessly over the few items of furniture that had been delivered over the past week.

There were the two long, deeply-cushioned sofas in dark green corded velvet, facing each other over the custom-made, polished oak coffee table. The bookcase, also in oak, the first of three ordered from the same craftsman. The thick cream rug, circular and luxurious that fronted the carved wooden fireplace.

A fairly minimal selection, yet all things they had chosen together, planning to add to them—over time.

Only there was no time. Not any more.

His throat muscles tightened to the point of

agony, and he dug his nails into the palms of his clenched hands to dam back the cry that threatened to burst from his lungs.

And down the hall, behind the closed door of that other room—the bed. Memories he could not allow himself to think about.

He wasn't even sure what he was doing here. Why he'd come back. God knows, it hadn't been his original intention.

Brendan and Grace had pressed him anxiously to go back and stay with them, but he couldn't face the thought of their shocked sympathy, however genuine and well-meant. Couldn't stomach the prospect of being treated as walking wounded. Or feeling the complete fool he undoubtedly was.

His mouth tightened as he remembered the barrage of cameras and shouted questions waiting for him outside the registry office as he walked alone down the steps. He'd been spared nothing, and tomorrow the papers would be full of it. The tabloids would probably feature him front page.

But there were issues that mattered far more than the destruction of what had become his cherished privacy.

Decisions would have to be made, of course. The furniture disposed of. The flat put back on the market. That was the easy part. It could be done at a distance by other people, in the same way that flights and reservations for a suite in an exclusive resort hotel in the Bahamas had already been cancelled. The special orders for flowers and champagne rescinded. The plans to charter a boat in order to visit some of the other islands shelved.

However, retrieving himself from the wreckage of his life would be a very different matter. But there he could at least make a start.

He turned and walked swiftly down the passage, to the room he'd designated as his working space. Not to be confused with the similar room next door, although both had been rudimentarily equipped with a desk and chair, a filing cabinet and a shredder.

He reached into his jacket pocket and extracted the crumpled sheet of paper which he'd carried with him since that morning. He did not attempt to read it again. There was no need. He could have recited its contents from memory—something else that must stop right here and now.

He unfolded the letter, put it down on the desk, smoothed it flat with his fist, then fed it into the shredder, which accepted the offering, reducing it to fragments with its swift high-pitched whine.

It was done. Now all he had to do was crase it

from his brain. Not so simple a task. But, somehow, he would manage it. Because he must.

He glanced at his watch. There was nothing more to keep him here. But then, there never had been. Waiting for him now was a different hotel suite, this one bland and anonymous. No intimate dinner for two to be anticipated, no vintage champagne on ice or rose petals on the pillows. And, later no eyes, drowsy with shared fulfilment, smiling into his.

Just a bottle of single malt, one glass, and, hopefully, oblivion.

At least until tomorrow when, somehow, he would begin his life again.

CHAPTER ONE

The previous April...

'BUT you don't understand. I'm meeting someone here.'

As the sound of the girl's voice, husky with desperation, reached him across the room, Caz Brandon
turned from the group he was chatting to at the
bar, and looked towards the door, his dark brows
raised in faint annoyance. Only to find his irrita-
tion changing in a flash to interest as he surveyed
the newcomer.

In her early to mid-twenties, he judged, medium
height, slim, and rather more than attractive, with
a mass of auburn hair falling in gleaming waves
past her shoulders. Wearing the ubiquitous little black dress, sleeveless and scoop-necked, like
many of the other female guests, but setting her
own stamp upon it with the slender skirt split almost to mid-thigh, revealing a black velvet garter set with crystals a few inches above her knee.

An intriguing touch, Caz decided with frank

appreciation. And one that offered grounds for speculation. Although, admittedly, this was hardly the time or the place to let his thoughts wander, however agreeably, when he was entertaining the European and Southern hemisphere editors who worked for his company, prior to the strategy meetings which would begin in the morning.

'I'm afraid this is a private function, madam, and your name is not on the list.' Jeff Stratton, who was handling security for the reception, spoke quietly but firmly.

'But I was invited.' She took a card from her evening purse. 'By this man—Phil Hanson. Look, he even wrote the place and the time for me to meet him on the back. If you'll just get him, he'll confirm what I say.'

Jeff shook his head. 'Unfortunately there is no Mr Hanson listed among those attending. I'm afraid someone may have been having a joke with you. However, I regret that I must still ask you to leave.'

'But he must be here.' There was real distress in her voice. 'He said he could get me a job with the Brandon Organisation. It's the only reason I agreed to come.'

Caz winced inwardly. The situation seemed to be morphing from a simple security glitch into a public relations problem. If someone had been making free with his company's name in order to play an unpleasant trick on this girl, he could hardly shrug and turn away. It had to be dealt with, and he, rather than Angus, who headed his PR team, was the one on the spot.

He excused himself smilingly to the rest of the group and walked purposefully across the room.

'Good evening,' he said. 'Miss…?' And paused interrogatively.

'Desmond,' she said, with a slight catch of the breath. 'Tarn Desmond.'

Seen at close hand, she was even lovelier than Caz had first thought, her green eyes over-bright as if tears were not too far away, and her creamy skin flushed with embarrassment. While her hair had the sheen of silk.

'And whom did you come here to meet?' he prompted gently. 'A Mr Hanson, you said? Did he claim a connection with the Brandon Organisation?'

She nodded. 'He said he worked for a Rob Wellington in Personnel. That he'd introduce me to him.'

Caz swore under his breath. This was getting worse all the time. He sent a silent signal to Jeff who melted unobtrusively away.

'I'm afraid we have no employee called Hanson.'
He paused. 'How well do you know this man?'

She bit her lip. 'Not very. I met him at a party a
few nights ago. We got talking and I mentioned
I was looking for a job. He said he might be able
to help, and gave me this card.' She added with
faint weariness, 'He seemed—nice.'

Caz gave the card a brief glance. It was a cheap
mass-produced thing, with the name Philip
Hanson printed in ostentatiously flowing letters,
but no other information, not even a mobile phone
number. But the time and place of this reception
was written quite unmistakably in capitals on the
back.

The deception was quite deliberate, he thought,
if inexplicable. Tarn Desmond had been sent here.

He said easily, 'Well, this is an awkward situation, Miss Desmond, but it doesn't have to become a crisis. I'm sincerely sorry that you should
have been misled like this but there's no need for
us to add to your disappointment.'

He paused again. 'You must allow me to make
amends. May I get you a drink?'

She hesitated, then shook her head. 'Thank you,
but it might be better if I did as your Rottweiler
asked—and simply left.'

Infinitely better, Caz thought wryly, at the same time aware of his own reluctance to see her go.

'But not totally empty-handed, I hope,' he said. 'If you want to work for the Brandon Organisation, why not contact Rob Wellington through the usual channels and see what's available?' He smiled at her, noting the beguiling fullness of her lower lip, and heard himself add, 'I'll make sure he's expecting to hear from you.'

The look that reached him from beneath the long, darkened lashes was frankly sceptical. Clearly, she didn't want to be made a fool of a second time, and who could blame her?

'Well—thank you again,' she said, and turned away. As she did so, a breath of the scent she wore reached him—soft, musky and sexy as hell, he decided as his senses stirred. And he was treated to another glimpse of the glittering crystals on that garter as she departed.

If she'd come here to make an impression, it had certainly worked on one level, he thought ruefully as he returned to the bar. But she would need better credentials than that to convince his Head of Personnel that she deserved a place in the company. Rob was in his forties, happily married, and quite impervious to the charms of other women, however young and alluring.

As for himself, thirty-four and conspicuously single, he needed to put the delectable Miss Desmond out of his mind, and get back to the serious business of the evening.

But that, he discovered, was not as easy as he thought. Like her perfume, she seemed to be lingering on the edge of his consciousness long after the reception was over, and he was back in his penthouse apartment, alone, with all the time in the world to think. And remember her.

Tarn walked into the flat, closed the door and leaned against it for a moment, eyes closed as she steadied her breathing, before crossing the hall to the living room.

Della, who owned the flat, was sitting on the floor absorbed in painting her toenails, but she glanced up at Tarn's entry, her expression enquiring and anxious. 'How did it go?'

'Like a breeze.' Tarn kicked off her high-heeled sandals and collapsed into a chair. 'Dell, I couldn't believe my luck. He was right there in the bar. I saw him as soon as I went in.'

She grinned exultantly. 'I didn't even have to get past security and go looking. And he was across almost as soon as I went into my spiel, oozing charm and concern. He swallowed every word, and wanted more. It was almost too easy.'

She took the card from her bag and tore it up. 'Goodbye, Mr Hanson, my imaginary acquaintance. You've been a great help, and well worth the effort of getting this printed.'

She looked back at Della. 'And thanks for the loan of the dress and this pretty thing.' She slipped off the garter and twirled it round her finger. 'It certainly hit the target.'

'Hmm.' Della pulled a face. 'I suppose I should congratulate you, but I still feel more like screaming "Don't do it".' She replaced the cap on her nail polish, and looked gravely up at her friend. 'It's not too late. You could still pull out and no harm done.'

'No harm?' Tarn sat up sharply. 'How can you say that? When Evie's in that dreadful place, with her whole life destroyed—and all because of him.'

'You're being a bit hard on The Refuge,' Della objected mildly. 'It has a tremendous reputation for dealing with all kinds of addictions as well as mental problems, so it's hardly a dreadful place. It's also very expensive,' she went on thoughtfully. 'So I'm surprised Mrs Griffiths can afford to keep her there.'

'Apparently they're obliged to take a quota of

National Health patients as well.' Tarn paused. 'And don't look so sceptical. Chameleon may have earned me a lot of money over the past few years, but not nearly enough to fund Evie at a top private clinic. I swear I'm not paying her fees.'

She drew a shuddering breath. 'When I came back and saw her there, realised the state she was in, I swore I'd make him pay for what he's done, and I shall, no matter how long it takes, or what the cost,' she concluded fiercely.

'Well, that's precisely it. You see, I was thinking of a totally different kind of harm,' Della returned, unperturbed. 'The potential cost to you.'

'What are you talking about?' Tarn was instantly defensive.

Della shrugged. 'I mean that when push comes to shove, you may not find it so simple to deliver the death blow and walk away, leaving the dagger in his back. Because you lack the killer instinct, my pet. Unlike, I've always thought, the eternally fragile Evie.'

She allowed that to sink in, then continued, 'For heaven's sake, Tarn, I know you're grateful to the Griffiths family for all they've done for you, but surely you've repaid them over and over again, financially and in every other way. Do you still have to come galloping to the rescue each time there's a problem? Surely there's a moment to say—"Halt, that's enough," and this could be it. For one thing, what about your career? Yes, the kind of work you do requires you to seem invisible. But you shouldn't actually become so in real life. You can't afford it. Have you thought of that?'

'I always take a break between projects,' Tarn returned. 'And by the time negotiations have been completed on the next deal, this will all be over, and I'll be back in harness.'

She looked down at her hands, clasped in her lap. 'Besides, I promised Uncle Frank before he died that I'd look after Aunt Hazel and Evie, just as he always looked after me. As I've told you, they only decided to become foster parents because they thought they couldn't have children of their own. Then, when Evie was born, they could have asked Social Services to take me away.'

She sighed. 'But they didn't, and I'm sure that was his doing rather than Aunt Hazel's. I was never the pretty docile little doll she'd always wanted. That became abundantly clear as I grew up. But I couldn't blame her. Looking back, I probably gave her a very hard time.

'But losing Uncle Frank knocked them both sideways. They were likc boats drifting on the tide, and they needed an anchor. I can't ignore them when they need help.'

'Well, if Evie reckoned on Caz Brandon becoming the family anchor in your place, she gravely miscalculated,' Della said with a touch of grimness. 'He isn't a man for serious relationships with women. In fact, he's famous for it, as you'd know if you hadn't been working abroad so much, and only back for flying visits. Evie, on the other hand, has been right here all the time, and should have been well aware that he's not the marrying kind.'

She hesitated. 'I'm playing devil's advocate here, but is it possible she may simply have— misunderstood his intentions?'

There was a silence, then Tarn said huskily, 'If so, it was because he meant her to do so. That's the unforgivable thing. Del—she's really suffering. She trusted that bastard, believed every lie he told her.' She shook her head.

'She may well have been incredibly naïve, but I've seen him in action now, and he's quite a piece of work. The arch-predator of the western world on the look-out for another victim.'

She gave a harsh laugh. 'My God, he even asked me to have a drink with him.'

'Which you naturally declined.'

'Yes, of course. It's much too soon for that.' Tarn's lips tightened. 'He's going to find out just what it's like to be strung along endlessly and then discarded like a piece of trash.'

'Well, for God's sake, be careful.' Della got to her feet. 'Caz Brandon may like to love them and leave them, but he's no fool. Don't forget he inherited a struggling publishing company seven years ago and has turned it into an international success.'

'The bigger they are,' said Tarn, 'the harder they fall. And his business achievements don't necessarily make him a decent human being. He needs to be taught that you can't simply take what you want and walk away. That eventually there's a price to be paid. And I intend to teach him precisely that.' She added tautly, 'For Evie's sake.'

'Then all I can say is—rather you than me,' said Della. 'And now I'm going to make some coffee.'

Left to herself, Tarn sank back against the cushions, trying to relax. She didn't really need coffee, she thought. She was hyped up quite enough as it was, the adrenalin still surging through her. And this was only the first stage of her plan.

The next big hurdle, of course, would be getting a job at the Brandon Organisation. This evening was a walk in the park compared with that.

But you can do it, she told herself robustly. There's a lot riding on this—the total and very public humiliation of Caz Brandon. In some way.

For a moment, the image of him filled her mind as completely as if he was standing there in front of her. Tall, broad-shouldered and elegant to his fingertips in his dinner jacket and black tie, his dark hair combed back from a lean incisive face. Hazel eyes, long-lashed under straight brows, a firm-lipped mouth, the nose and chin strongly marked.

Oh, yes, she thought savagely. She could see why Evie had fallen for him so far and so fast. With very little effort, he could probably be—irresistible.

And she gave a sudden shiver.

She'd been in New York when Aunt Hazel's call had come, she recalled later that night, when sleep remained curiously elusive.

'Tarn—Tarn—are you there—or is it just that nasty machine?'

She'd known at once from the agitated tone that it meant trouble. In any case, her foster mother rarely rang just for a catch-up chat. And lately there'd been hardly any calls at all, Aunt Hazel, she'd supposed, being totally preoccupied by preparations for Evie's forthcoming and presumably triumphant marriage.

She said briskly, 'Yes, I'm here. What's the matter?'

'It's Evie. Oh, God, Tarn.' The words were tumbling over each other. 'My poor baby. She's taken an overdose of sleeping pills—tried to kill herself.'

Tarn heard her with horrified dismay. Evie might be something of a flake at times, but attempted suicide? That was unbelievable. Awful beyond words.

'Tarn—did you hear what I said?'

'I heard,' Tarn said slowly. 'But why should she do such a thing? In her letters, she always seemed so happy.'

'Well, she's not happy now, not any more.' Aunt Hazel was crying with loud, breathy sobs. 'Perhaps never again. Because he's finished with her—that man—that brute she was going to marry. The engagement's off and she's had a complete nervous collapse as a result. She's been rushed into some kind of rest home, and they won't allow visitors. Not even me.

'Tarn, I'm going frantic. You've got to come home. I can't be alone at a time like this. I may go to pieces myself. You have to find out what's going on at this place—The Refuge. They might talk to you. You're so good at this kind of thing.'

Except, Tarn thought grimly, that would-be suicides and mental breakdowns were well outside her experience zone.

She said gently, 'Don't worry, Aunt Hazel. I'll get the first available flight. But you shouldn't be on your own. Would Mrs Campbell stay with you till I get there?'

'Oh, no,' the older woman said quickly. 'You see I'd have to explain—and I can't. No-one else knew about the wedding, apart from us. It was all going to be a totally hush-hush affair. And if Mrs Campbell ever found out, she'd tell everyone that my poor girl's been jilted, and I couldn't bear that.'

'Hush-hush?' Tarn repeated astonished. 'But why?'

'Because that's the way they both wanted it. No fuss.' Mrs Griffiths was crying again. 'Who could have thought it would end like this?'

Who indeed? Tarn thought grimly as she eventually replaced the receiver. And why on earth would the head of publishing conglomerate the Brandon Organisation want his forthcoming marriage to be a secret? Unless, of course, there was never going to be any marriage—and that was another secret that, this time, he'd carefully kept to himself.

Because St Margaret's Westminster and an all-day party at the Savoy or some other glamorous venue, accompanied by all the razzmatazz at his disposal seemed more the style for a billionaire tycoon.

Not that many of them crossed her path very often, she reminded herself wryly.

She still found it almost impossible to credit what had happened. It was true that her foster mother had always been an emotional woman, and prone to exaggeration yet this time there seemed every excuse for her reaction.

She wandered restlessly round her loft apartment, as she considered what to do.

A flight to Heathrow for the following day was, of course, her main priority. But she had also to deal with the problem of Howard, who would not be pleased to hear that she wouldn't be accompanying him to the Florida Keys to stay with some friends he had there.

Tarn herself had mixed feelings about the cancellation of the trip. She and Howard had been dating for a while now, but she'd been careful to keep their relationship as casual and platonic as all the others she'd embarked on in the past. Not that there'd been that many.

However, she recognised that this state of affairs could probably not be maintained indefinitely. This invitation was clearly intended to move things to a more intimate level, and she'd accepted, mainly because she could think of no good reason to refuse.

Howard Brenton worked as management editor with Van Hilden International, the company which published the celebrity 'biographies' which Tarn now so successfully ghosted under her company name 'Chameleon'. Which was how they'd met.

He was attractive, amusing and available (three starred A's on the Manhattan scene). Tarn liked him, but wasn't sure if love would ever be on the cards. But, she'd eventually decided, perhaps it deserved to be given at least a fighting chance.

After all, what was she waiting for? she'd asked herself with faint cynicism. Prince Charming to gallop up on a white horse, like Evie, who'd been sending her letter after letter rhapsodising over the manifold perfections of Caz Brandon, the man she was going to marry?

But now it seemed that her own warier approach

was the right one because Evie's idol had proved to have feet of clay.

She shook her head in angry bewilderment. How could it all have gone so wrong? And, apparently, so fast? Evie's last screed, cataloguing in some detail her future husband's numerous acts of generosity and tenderness had arrived just over a week ago, indicating that her path in life would be strewn with roses. Tarn would have sworn there wasn't a single doubt in her mind.

Yet there must have been something, she thought. Some small clue, some hint she could trace that would signal all wasn't well. And if there was, then she would find it.

She booked her flight, left a message on Howard's voicemail, suggesting they meet for a drink in their favourite bar as soon as he finished work, then went across to her desk.

She opened a drawer and extracted Evie's letters, collected into a bundle, and secured by a rubber band.

There were a lot of them, each envelope containing page after page of ecstatic outpourings from Evie's first meeting with Caz Brandon in a classic secretary/boss situation down to what had probably been the last, she thought biting her lip, and she wasn't altogether sure why she'd kept them.

Unless she'd believed they were some kind of proof that fairy tales can come true. If so, how wrong was it possible to be?

Evie, she thought, had always been a great one for writing things down. As well as the mass bombardment of letters, she'd kept a diary since she was a small child, and later produced reams of poetry to celebrate the girlhood crush of the moment.

She made herself a beaker of tea, settled into her favourite cream leather recliner and began to read.

'I've got the most fantastic job working for the most fantastic man,' Evie had written in her swift, untidy scrawl, the words leaping off the page. 'His regular secretary is away on maternity leave, so, hopefully, I'm in for the duration. And after that—who knows?'

Ironically, Tarn could remember feeling relieved that Evie had finally found work that suited her, and also thinking with amusement that all it had taken was a good-looking boss.

Evie's next letter was a fairly bread and butter affair, but the one after that bubbled with excitement. The boss from heaven had asked her to work through her lunch hour, and had ordered a platter of sandwiches which he'd shared with her.

Well, what was he supposed to do—eat them in front of her? Tarn muttered under her breath.

'He was asking me all sorts of questions about myself—my interests—my ambitions.' Evie had gone on. 'He's just so easy to talk to. And he smiles with his eyes.'

I just bet he does, thought Tarn. She recalled smiling herself over Evie's raptures the first time around. But how could she ever have found them amusing?

Curiosity had led her to look at Caz Brandon on the Internet, and she had to admit he was everything Evie had said and possibly more. But why couldn't I see what he really was? she asked herself as she read on. A cynical womaniser playing with a vulnerable girl's emotions.

Over the next week, Evie's hero stopped being Mr Brandon and became Caz instead.

'Caz took me for a drink after work at this fabulous wine bar,' Evie confided in her next effusion. 'It was simply heaving with celebrities and media people and I was introduced to them all. I didn't know whether I was on my head or my heels.'

After that, the invitation to dinner seemed almost inevitable. Evie gave a description of the restaurant in total detail—the décor, the service, every course they'd eaten and the wine he'd chosen.

Like a child in a toyshop, Tarn thought, sighing.

And the toys kept on coming. There were more dinners for two, plus theatre visits, concerts and even film premieres.

Then, eventually, there was the weekend at a romantic inn in the depths of the countryside.

'Of course I can't go on working for him,' Evie had written. 'Caz has this strict rule about not mixing business with pleasure, and he says I'm all pleasure. So I'm being transferred to another department.

'He's also arranging for me to move into my own flat so that we can be together whenever we wish, but I'll be protected from people gossiping and drawing the wrong conclusions.

'I know now what the marriage service means by "to love and to cherish", because that's how Caz is with me.'

A gap of a few weeks followed, while the loving and cherishing presumably continued apace, then Evie wrote again.

'Tarn, we're engaged. He's bought me the most beautiful ring—a huge diamond cluster. It must have cost an absolute fortune, and shows how much he must love me. I'm only sorry I can't wear it to work, but I realise that would hardly be discreet.

'I can hardly believe he's chosen me. All his other girlfriends have been so glamorous and famous. But, by some miracle, I'm the one he wants to spend the rest of his life with.'

Well, it was feasible, Tarn had told herself, dismissing her instinctive uneasiness about this whirlwind courtship. Evie was pretty enough to catch anyone's eye, and her lack of sophistication might come as a welcome relief to a man accustomed to high-powered women.

'His flat is wonderful,' the letter had continued. 'A big penthouse with views all over London, and an amazing collection of modern art. I don't pretend to understand all of it, but he says he'll teach me when we're married.

'And he has the most incredible bed I've ever seen—Emperor sized at the very least. I tease him that he may lose me in it, but he says there's no danger of that. That however far away I went, he'd find me. Isn't that wonderful?'

Not the word I'd have chosen, thought Tarn, dropping the closely written sheet as if it had burned her fingers. Or not any more. 'Hooked and reeled in' now seemed far more apposite.

The letters that followed were full of wedding

plans, the chosen dress, flowers and possible hon-eymoon destinations, which Tarn had glossed over at the first reading. Now they assumed an almost unbearable poignancy.

And finally, 'Being with Caz is like having all my sweetest dreams come true. How can I be so lucky?'

Only Evie's luck had changed, and she'd sud-denly discovered what a short step it was from dream to nightmare. So much so, that the thought of life without him had become impossible, and she'd tried to end it.

Tarn sat staring down at the mass of paper in her lap. She thought of Evie, wisp-slender, with her unruly mass of blonde hair and huge blue eyes, the unexpected late-born child, her flaws excused, her foibles indulged. Adored and cos-seted for the whole of her life. Expecting no less from the man who, for reasons of his own, had professed to love her.

How blatantly, unthinkingly cruel was that?

Her throat was tight and she wanted very much to cry, but that would not help Evie. Instead she needed to stay strong and feed the smouldering knot of anger deep within her, bringing it to full flame.

She said aloud, her voice cold and clear, 'You've

destroyed her, you bastard. But you're not going to get away with it. Because, somehow, I'm going to do exactly the same to you.'

Several weeks on, the words still echoed in her head. And tonight, thought Tarn as she punched her pillow into shape and curled into the mattress. Tonight she'd taken the first real step on the path to Caz Brandon's ultimate downfall.

CHAPTER TWO

THE REFUGE was a large redbrick house in Georgian style, standing in several acres of landscaped grounds.

As she'd approached it on her first visit, Tarn, seeing the people sitting around the lawns in the sunshine, had thought it resembled an exclusive country house hotel, until she realised just how many of those present were wearing the white tunics and trousers of medical staff.

And, as she got inside, the illusion of peace and comfort was completely destroyed. She'd known that permission for her to see Evie had been given reluctantly, but she'd not expected to be taken into a small room leading off the imposing tiled hall, obliged to hand over her shoulder bag and informed tersely it would be returned to her when she left, or have to submit to a swift search before being taken upstairs to be interviewed by Professor Wainwright, the clinical director.

And her protest about the way she'd been treated

cut no ice with the grey-haired bearded man facing her across a large desk.

'Our concern is with the well-being and safety of the men and women in our care, Miss Griffiths, and not your sensitivities,' he told her tersely.

Tarn decided not to argue over her surname and looked him coldly in the eye. 'You cannot imagine for one moment that I would wish to harm my sister.'

He opened the file lying in front of him. 'Your foster sister, I believe.'

'Does it make a difference?'

'It's one of the aspects of her case that have to be considered,' he returned, and paused. 'You understand the conditions of your visit, I trust.'

Tarn bit her lip. 'I am not to question her about what happened or the events leading up to it,' she responded neutrally. *Not that I have to as her own letters have told me all I need to know. But I don't have to tell you that.*

She added quietly, 'Nor am I to apply any pressure on her to confide in me about her treatment here.'

'Correct.' He looked at her over the top of his rimless glasses. 'It is unfortunate that we have had to temporarily exclude her mother from visiting Miss Griffiths, but it was felt that she is an excitable and over-emotional woman and her presence could be less than helpful.'

'Is anyone else allowed to see her?'

'No-one.' He closed the file. 'This may be reviewed if and when she begins to make progress.' He pressed a buzzer. 'Nurse Farlow will take you to her.'

At the door, she paused. 'I brought my sister some of her favourite chocolate truffles. They were in the bag that was taken from me. I'd still like her to have them.'

'I'm afraid she is not allowed presents of food at the moment. In future you should check whether any proposed gifts are permitted.'

It was more like a prison than a clinic, Tarn thought, as a sturdy blonde woman escorted her silently through a maze of corridors. And they seemed to be treating Evie more as a criminal than a patient.

Didn't they understand what had happened here? How Evie had been used by this rich bastard then callously dumped when he'd got all he wanted and become bored? How her attempted suicide was an act of total desperation?

When they eventually halted at a door, the nurse gave Tarn a warning glance. 'This first visit is for fifteen minutes only,' she informed her brusquely. 'At the end of this time, I'll be back to collect you.'

She opened the door, said, 'Someone to see you, dear,' and urged Tarn forward.

Tarn had almost expected a cell with bars on the window. Instead she found herself in a pleasant bedroom with modern furnishings, seascape prints on the neutral walls, and soft blue curtains. Evie was in bed, propped against a pile of pillows with her eyes closed, and Tarn almost recoiled in shock at the sight of her.

Her fair hair was lank, her face was haggard and her body looked almost shrunken under the blue bedspread.

Thank God they've kept Aunt Hazel away, Tarn thought, swallowing, or she'd be having permanent hysterics. I feel like bursting into tears myself.

There were a pair of small armchairs flanking the window and Tarn moved one of them nearer the bed, and sat down.

For several minutes there was silence, then Evie said hoarsely, 'Caz? Oh, Caz, is it you? Are you here at last?'

For a moment, Tarn was unable to speak, shaken by a wave of anger mixed with pity. Then she reached out and took the thin hand, saying quietly, 'No, love. It's only me.'

Evie's eyelids lifted slowly. Her eyes looked strangely pale, as if incessant crying had somehow washed away their normal colour.

She gave a little sigh. 'Tarn—I knew you'd come. You've got to get me out of here. They won't let me leave, even though I keep asking. They say if I want to get better, I have to forget Caz. Forget how much I loved him. Accept that it's all over between us. But I can't—I can't.

'They give me things—to help me relax, they say. To make me sleep, but I dream about him, Tarn. Dream that he's still mine.'

Her fingers closed fiercely round Tarn's. 'I didn't want to go on living without him. Couldn't face another day with nothing left to hope for. You understand that, don't you? You must, because you knew what he meant to me. How I built my future around him.'

Tarn said steadily, 'I suppose so, but ending it all was never the answer, believe me.' She paused. 'Evie, you're a very beautiful girl, and one day you'll meet another man—someone good and decent who'll appreciate you and genuinely want to spend his life with you.'

'But I wanted Caz.' Her grip on Tarn's hand

tightened almost unbearably. 'I gave him every-thing. So how could he reject me like that? Not want me to love him any more?'

'I don't know.' Tarn freed herself gently. 'But we mustn't talk about that now or you'll get agi-tated and they'll know. Which means I won't be allowed to see you again.'

'And you're all I've got.' Evie sank back against her pillows, her face white and pinched. 'Because Caz is never going to come here, is he? I've been hoping and hoping, but it isn't going to happen. I know that now.'

A slow tear ran down her cheek. 'How could he do this to me? How can he just—walk away as if I didn't matter?'

Tarn felt the anger rising inside her again, and curled her nails into the palms of her hands to re-gain her control.

'But you do matter,' she said, her voice shaking. 'And one day soon he's going to find out just how much, and be sorrier than he's ever imagined.'

She handed Evie a tissue from the box on the bedside table. 'Now dry your eyes, and try to look as if my visit has done you some good. And next time I come we'll talk seriously about how to deal with Mr Caz Brandon.'

* * *

That night over supper, she said, 'So what did you think of Evie's fiancé, Aunt Hazel? Did you ever feel that things weren't quite right between them?'

Her foster mother put down her knife and fork and stared at her. 'But I never met him,' she said. 'I knew only what Evie told me, and, of course, she absolutely worshipped him.'

'Never met him?' Tarn repeated slowly. 'But how can that be? You mean she never brought him home?'

'Well, she'd hardly be likely to,' Mrs Griffiths said with a touch of defensiveness. 'I mean—he lives in the lap of luxury, and this is such an ordinary little house. But they were planning to give an enormous party when their engagement was announced, and I was going to meet him then.'

'I see,' said Tarn, without any truth whatsoever. She hesitated. 'And you were all right with this?'

'As long as my girl was happy, I was too,' said Mrs Griffiths with finality, and the subject was ostensibly dropped.

But it provided Tarn with food for thought during the remainder of the evening.

When Tarn returned to The Refuge a few days later, she was surprised to be accorded a wintry smile by the Professor.

'I think you will find your sister has improved slightly. She is looking forward to seeing you again.' He paused. 'But you will have to remain her only visitor in the immediate future. Have you brought her any messages from anyone else? If so, may I know what they are?'

'Her mother sends her love.' Tarn lifted her chin. 'I hope that's acceptable.'

There was another slight hesitation before he said, 'Perfectly,' and buzzed for Nurse Farlow.

Evie, in a dressing gown, was sitting in the arm-chair by the window. Her newly washed hair was waving softly round her face, and her face had re-gained some colour.

'Wow.' Tarn bent and kissed her on the cheek. 'You'll be out of here in no time at this rate.'

'I wish,' Evie said with a sigh. 'But there's no chance. That's been made perfectly clear to me. It's what happens when you do crazy things. And all because of him.' She punched her fist into the palm of her other hand. 'That was the real mad-ness—to believe even one word that he said. To trust him. I ought to have realised he was just using me.'

Her voice cracked. 'Oh, God, he's the one I should have tried to kill for what he's done—not myself. You talked about making him sorry.

That's not enough. I want to make him wish he was dead.'

'Well, maybe we can.' Tarn took the chair opposite. 'But stay calm, honey, because there are some things I need to know from you.'

Evie stared at her, biting her lip. 'What kind of things?'

'Stuff you might have told him. About your mother. About me.'

There was a silence, then Evie said, 'I didn't tell him anything. He never wanted to talk about family things.'

'You didn't find that—odd?' Tarn spoke carefully.

'It was the way he was.' Evie shrugged. 'I accepted it. Why do you ask?'

'Because it helps if he doesn't know I exist. When I meet him, he won't be on his guard.'

'You're going to meet him?' Evie was suddenly rigid, her colour fading. 'No, you can't. You mustn't. You—you don't know what he's like.'

'But that's exactly what I'm going to find out,' Tarn told her. 'I need to know everything about him, because, in order to damage him, I have to discover his Achilles' heel—and he will have one. Everyone does.'

She paused. 'You're sure you never mentioned me? Told him my name?'

'No, never.' Evie shook her head slowly. 'Why would I?' She gave a quick shiver. 'All the same, keep away from him, Tarn. It—it's not safe. He has powerful friends.'

'I won't take any unnecessary risks. The fact that he has no idea who I am gives me a head start.' Tarn tried to sound reassuring, even if she was bewildered by Evie's warning. Surely Caz Brandon was powerful enough on his own. 'But if I'm to cause him the kind of pain he's inflicted on you, I have to get close to him in some way. Find where the wound will be deepest.'

'You imagine you can do that?' Evie whispered. 'Then perhaps you're the crazy one. Not me.'

'I can at least try,' Tarn returned. She hesitated. 'I'm not going to mention any of this to your mother. And you shouldn't talk about it either, to anyone. It has to be our secret.

'Also, I shall move out of Wilmont Road,' she added. 'Go to stay with a friend.'

'You mean it, don't you? You're really going to do this.' Evie shifted restively in her chair, her face taut, almost frightened. 'Oh, I wish I'd never mentioned him.' She added pettishly, 'Now, I'm starting to get a headache. Perhaps it would be better if you left.'

'Yes, of course.' Tarn got to her feet, eying her with concern. She said gently, 'Evie—this man has to be taught he can't go through life trampling on people. What he did to you had almost fatal results, and I cannot forget that. You're in no position to fight back, but I am.'

She tried a coaxing smile. 'And you really don't have to worry.'

'You don't think so?' Evie hunched a shoulder and turned to stare blankly at the window. 'That's because you don't know him.' And she shivered again.

It was her hair that Caz recognised. Even though it was no longer cascading to her shoulders, but decorously confined in a neat braid, and tied with a navy bow which matched her neat pantsuit, there was no mistaking that glorious rich auburn.

He had never really expected to see her again, yet here she was just the same, entering the lift at the fifth floor, glancing at her Blackberry with a preoccupied frown, and apparently quite oblivious to everything else.

He said, 'It's Miss Desmond, isn't it?'

She looked up with a start. 'Oh,' she said, and

bit her lip. 'It's you.' She paused. 'I'm so sorry I didn't realise who you were the other evening, Mr Brandon. I feel seriously embarrassed.'

'Don't worry about it.' Caz paused, his mouth relaxing into amusement. 'But while I have no wish to add to your discomfort, I should perhaps point out this is the directors' private lift, and, if spotted, you could get told off for using it.'

'Oh, Lord.' She pulled a face. 'I think that was mentioned, but I forgot and just took the first one to arrive. I apologise again.'

'Do I take it you're working here now?'

She nodded. 'Since Monday.' Her sidelong glance was part shy, part mischievous. 'I actually took your advice and applied through the proper channels. Mr Wellington was good enough to hire me—temporarily anyway.'

She paused. 'Should I get out at the first floor, or travel to ground level and risk a reprimand?'

'Stay on board,' he said. 'If anyone notices, refer them to me, and I'll tell them we were renewing an old acquaintance.'

'Ah,' she said and pressed a button on the display. 'I think the stairs might be more discreet.' She added, 'Sir.'

As the doors opened, she gave him a last brief smile and vanished.

There should be a law, Caz mused, banning girls with legs as good as hers from wearing trousers in the office. Just as there was almost certainly a law condemning his thoughts as a kind of passive sexual harassment, he thought, his mouth curling in self-derision.

Easy, boy, he told himself. Or you'll break your own golden rule about non-fraternisation. And we can't have that.

If you need female distraction, ring Ginny Fraser, and see if she's free for dinner.

He did, and she was, and that should have been the end of it.

Yet, later over lunch in the executive dining room, he heard himself saying, his tone deliberately casual, 'I bumped into your newest recruit today, Rob.'

'I hardly deserve the credit for that,' his Personnel Chief said drily. 'You did tell me we might receive an application from her. I simply—took the hint.'

Caz stared at him, appalled. 'Oh, God, surely not.'

Rob Wellington grinned. 'No, don't worry. Absolutely not. Laurie interviewed her first, then sent me a note saying she was frantically over-qualified for any of our vacancies, but we'd be mad to pass her up on that account. I had a chat with the lady and agreed. So at the moment, she's working as editorial assistant in features and fiction on All Your Own covering Susan Ellis's maternity leave.'

He poured himself some more coffee. 'Anyway, judging by the reference we got from Hannah Strauss at Uptown Today in New York, Ms Desmond could easily be running the entire magazine single-handed.'

Caz's brows lifted. 'If she was such a success in Manhattan, how come she's back in London, at the bottom of the ladder again and working for comparative peanuts?' he asked sceptically. 'It makes no sense.'

'I asked her about that,' said Rob. 'She said she'd come home because of illness in the family, and decided to stay for a while.' He paused. 'I have to say she seemed extremely eager to work for us. Should we suspect her motives for any reason?'

'Maybe we should simply be flattered.' Caz thought for a moment. 'Do you know anything about a Philip Hanson? Have we ever employed anyone of that name in any capacity, however briefly?'

Rob frowned. 'Off-hand, I'd say no. But I can check our records.'

Caz pushed back his chair and rose. 'Forget

it,' he said. 'It's not that important, and you have enough to do.'

And I, he told himself, will also dismiss the whole business from my mind.

And as a positive move in this direction, when he got back to his office, he asked Robyn, his PA, to send Ginny Fraser some flowers.

Tarn switched off her computer and leaned back in her chair, flexing her shoulders wearily. It had been a fraught few hours, but she knew the task she'd been set was a job well done, and would be recognised as such.

How odd, she thought, that I should care.

Yet, in other circumstances, she knew she might have enjoyed her time on All Your Own. Working on her own as she did now, she'd almost forgotten the buzz of office life. Her colleagues were friendly and professional, and she liked the editor, Lisa Hastings, another recent appointment.

In fact she'd been the first to hear Lisa's cry of anguish as she scanned the pages of script that had just been handed to her.

'Oh, God—someone please tell me this is a joke.'

'What's happened?' Tarn had asked Kate who was in charge of the magazine's layout.

Kate cast her eyes to heaven. 'You've heard of Annetta Carmichael, the soap star? Apparently, when they killed her off as the Christmas Day ratings booster, she decided to take up a new career as a writer, and she's been offered megabucks for her first novel, a searing exposé of the secret world of television. A woman's fight to maintain her integrity against a sordid background of tragedy and betrayal.'

She grinned. 'You can practically hear the axe being ground. However, Brigid, Lisa's predecessor, thought it would be a great idea to commission a short story from her for an equally generous payment. I think the finished product has finally arrived, well after its deadline, and well short of the required standard.'

'I'd like to throw it back at her and tell her to start again,' Lisa was saying savagely. 'But she's pushed off to some Caribbean hideaway with someone else's husband, and is, according to her agent, incommunicado.'

She slammed the pages down on her desk. 'And we need this. It's already been announced—"Annetta—Fiction's Latest Find."' She snorted. 'Fiction's greatest disaster if this is anything to go by.'

'What's wrong with it?' Tarn asked.

'You mean apart from a poor beginning, a boring middle, and a hopeless ending?' Lisa gave a groan. 'It needs an instant re-write, but it's my little boy's birthday today and I swore to my husband that I would be back in plenty of time for the celebrations. I should have known something would crop up and ruin things.'

Tarn hesitated. 'Would you like me to take a look at it?' she asked diffidently. 'I have done stuff like this in the past, and it would give you a chance to get off as planned.'

Lisa stared at her in open surprise. 'Are you serious? Because anything you could do—even if it was just sorting out her spelling and grammar—would be a tremendous help.'

Back at her desk, Tarn gave a silent whistle as she looked through the pages. Everything Lisa had said was perfectly justified, she thought grimly. It was a genuine horror.

But she remembered all the endless reams of frightful autobiography, and the rambling taped reminiscences that she'd transformed into readable—and saleable—prose in the recent past.

This at least had the benefit of being short. And, buried inside, were the actual bones of a story.

I've never ghosted fiction before, she thought.

This will be a challenge. But I'll have the new draft done when Lisa arrives tomorrow.

The offices were beginning to empty as she began. By the time she'd completed the story to her own satisfaction, boosted by regular visits to the coffee machine, the building was dark and still, with only the occasional security patrols to disturb her concentration.

She printed off the new version, clipped the sheets together and took them to Lisa's work station.

She returned slowly to her seat, tucking her white blouse neatly back into her grey skirt as she went, then sat down to finish her final cup of coffee.

She was tired and hungry too, having eaten nothing since her mid-day sandwich. But she felt a curious sense of satisfaction all the same.

Just as if I was a bona fide employee, she thought wryly.

But then, she reflected, she'd had little opportunity to be anything else. Since she'd manufactured that meeting in the executive lift two weeks earlier, she hadn't managed to set eyes on Caz Brandon, even in passing.

She'd been aware, without conceit, that he'd again found her attractive, but there'd been no follow-up on his part, and office gossip said that he and TV presenter Ginny Fraser were a serious item.

Besides, she'd also been told, he never played around at the office. Which just showed, she'd thought angrily, how little they knew. But which also demonstrated that he must have wanted Evie very badly. And if he'd betrayed his own dubious principles once, he could surely be induced to do so again.

However, it was all a bit like the old recipe for Jugged Hare, which began 'First catch your hare...'

It was also time to visit Evie again, but she would have preferred to wait until she had something positive to report. And heaven only knows how long that will take, she told herself with a sigh.

She slipped on the black jacket hanging on the back of her chair, picked up her bag, and went to the double glass doors, using her security code to activate them.

As she walked down the corridor to the lifts, a man's familiar voice said, 'Doing overtime, Miss Desmond?'

Tarn whirled with a gasp, her bag crashing to

the floor, as startled as if a ghost had suddenly materialised in front of her.

Only moments before, she'd been asking herself quite seriously if she was wasting her time, and should jettison all thoughts of revenge and simply resume her own life. Now here was Caz Brandon appearing out of nowhere in this otherwise deserted building, as if her thoughts had conjured him up out of thin air.

She said huskily, 'You frightened me.'

'I got a hell of a shock too when I came back to pick up my briefcase and saw there were lights on this floor,' he returned tersely. 'What are you doing here at this time of night?'

'As you said—overtime.' Tarn dropped to one knee and began to retrieve the objects that had fallen out of her bag. 'But don't worry. It's the voluntary, unpaid kind. I had a project I was keen to finish.'

'Keen isn't the word,' he said drily. He picked up a lipstick that had rolled to his feet and handed it back to her. 'Aren't there enough hours in the working day for you? And haven't you got better things to do with your evenings than hang around here?'

'Most of the time, yes,' Tarn told him coolly as she rose and fastened her bag. 'This was a one-off.'

She was playing it all wrong, she knew, but his unexpected arrival had flustered her badly.

Also she felt scruffy in the clothes she'd been wearing all day, and wished she'd put on some more lipstick or at least freshened her scent.

He, on the other hand, looked unruffled and elegant in a dark suit and crimson silk tie.

This is my golden opportunity, she thought. Another one may never come my way and I'll have simply wasted the last weeks of my life. I've rehearsed this scenario so many times, yet suddenly, ridiculously, I can't think what to say. What to do.

He said abruptly, 'You look tired. When did you last eat?'

'I had lunch.' That should have been a come-on, but all she sounded was defensive.

'Then I'll take you out for some food, and a drink. There's a little Italian place I use that stays open till all hours.'

'No—please. I'm fine.' Dear God, this was a Rubicon moment but her brain didn't seem to be working properly. She rallied. 'I really can't put you to so much trouble.'

He shrugged. 'You're not.' His tone was laconic. 'If you like, consider it a reward for loyalty above and beyond the call of duty.' He paused. 'So, shall we go?'

And she heard herself say, in a voice she hardly recognised, 'In that case—yes—please.'

CHAPTER THREE

THIS was what she had wanted, had tried so un-
availingly to plan for, Tarn realised with a kind
of wonderment as she walked beside him down
the lamplit street. Yet now it had so unexpectedly
fallen into her lap, every instinct she possessed
was telling her to run away. Fast.

As they approached the kerb, she stumbled
slightly and his hand shot out and took her arm.

'Be careful,' he cautioned as he steadied her,
the warmth and firmness of his clasp seeming to
penetrate the fabric of her jacket.

She muttered a word of thanks, longing to
wrench herself free but not daring to, furious at
her own clumsiness and bitterly aware of the harsh
inner tensions which had caused it. Conscious too
that, in spite of her dislike of him, her skin was
tingling at his touch.

Oh, I'll be careful, she thought, the breath catching in her throat. My God, I will!

They crossed a road, then another, before walking the fifty odd yards down a side street to the Trattoria Giuliana.

It was busy, the hum of laughter and conversation quietly relaxed and delectable smells of herbs and garlic pervading the atmosphere. Caz was warmly greeted by the smiling proprietor and they were immediately shown to a corner table, where two glasses of *prosecco* were placed in front of them.

To her shame, Tarn realised her mouth was watering.

Caz raised his glass. *'Salute.'*

She returned the toast haltingly, glad when menus soon followed and she could focus on something other than the man watching her with frank intensity across the table.

Get a grip, she castigated herself, as she scanned the listed dishes. If he finds you attractive, make the most of it. If he was anyone else, you'd be relishing the situation and wondering how soon you could begin to flirt a little.

And all this talk of him avoiding office entanglements is just garbage. Evie wasn't a one-off. He's making that perfectly clear right now.

But if he's to suffer as much as he deserves, then you need him to be more than simply attracted to you. He has to want you so badly that it's like a sickness with him. A sickness for which you will never provide the cure.

And you're used to keeping men at arms' length. You've been doing it since adolescence. You can manage it again for as long as it's necessary.

Besides, he's the boss and you're just a lowly handmaid toiling on one of the Brandon Organisation's many publications, so you have every excuse for maintaining a respectful distance. But, it's also time to move from awkward to friendly.

She sighed lightly and looked at him her eyes smiling under her sweep of lashes. 'I seem to be spoiled for choice. As you eat here regularly, what can you recommend?'

He returned her smile. 'If you don't object to veal, the *Saltimbocca Romagna* is usually excellent.'

'I have no real hang-ups about food,' she said. 'I'll have it, with the *gnocchi* to start.'

'And I'll have the same, but begin with the wild mushroom risotto.'

He gave the order, and they agreed on a bottle of Friulano to go with it.

'So,' he said when the waiter had departed, leaving bowls of olive oil and chunks of bread to dip into them on the table. 'You seem to be enjoying your work on All Your Own. How do you rate it as a magazine?'

Tarn thought for a moment, then nodded. 'I'd say it hits most of its targets.'

'It certainly used to,' he said drily. 'However, the previous editor was keen on attracting a much younger readership.' He drank some *prosecco*. 'The numbers took a dive as a result.'

'Ah,' she said. 'So that's why I've been re-writing Annetta's story. It was intended for the youth market.'

'Re-writing?' His brows lifted. 'Is that within an assistant's remit?'

'Anything would have been an improvement on the original submission,' Tarn said, mentally kicking herself. 'But Lisa will naturally do the final draft.'

'I wasn't being critical. I'm seriously impressed.' He pushed a bowl of herb-flavoured oil closer to her. 'Try this with some bread. You look ready to fade away with hunger.'

His caring side, thought Tarn, fighting down cold fury as she tasted and made appreciative noises. And it was certainly a lovely restaurant, its tables far enough apart for privacy and set with snowy cloths, gleaming silver and crystal. But its air of quiet luxury was enhanced by a good atmosphere, and later arrivals than themselves were being accorded the same friendly welcome.

I wonder if this was where he brought Evie—that first time, she thought. If he also suggested to her what she might order. Asked if she was enjoying her work.

And Evie would have lapped it up. Unused to places like this, she would have gazed around her, getting more excited by the minute. Unable to believe how lucky she was to be in this glamorous restaurant with this equally glamorous man.

Everything about him spoke money—the exquisite tailoring, the expensive shirt, the plain platinum wristwatch. And all this, allied to the aura of power he carried so effortlessly, added up to a lethal combination.

She was like a lamb to the slaughter, Tarn thought bitterly. And he's probably used the same first date script with me as he did with her—learned by heart and used to decide whether the girl rates a follow-up rendezvous.

And I have to make it imperative for him to see me again—and not just by accident next time, but because he can't keep away.

He said reflectively, 'Tarn. That's a very lovely name—and unusual too.'

'Yes,' she said. 'A little too much so, I used to

think. There can't be many girls called after a mountain lake, so naturally, when I went to school, I got re-christened "Drippy".'

His brows lifted. 'Anyone less so I've yet to meet. What did you do?'

'Nothing.' Tarn shrugged. 'Just pretended I hadn't heard and didn't care. But the name stuck and followed me from year to year. I hoped they'd get tired of the joke but they didn't.'

He pulled a face. 'Kids can be monsters. Have you ever told your parents what they put you through and extracted a grovelling apology?'

'No,' she said. 'I never did.' And paused. 'Anyway, where did Caz come from?'

He sighed. 'You're not the only sufferer. I was born on January the Sixth and my mother insisted I should be called after one of the three Kings, and fortunately she picked Caspar over Melchior and Balthazar or I should have been in even more trouble.'

He smiled at her. 'So that's the first thing we have in common.'

'And probably the one and only.' She managed to infuse her tone with a note of faint regret.

'Why do you say that?'

'Isn't it obvious?' She shrugged again. 'You own the company. I work for it.'

'And you find that an insuperable obstacle in the way of our better acquaintance?'

'I think it has to be.' She gave him a reflective look. 'And if you're honest, so do you.'

Except honesty isn't really your thing, is it, Mr Mighty Publishing Tycoon?

He spoke slowly, his lean, brown fingers toying with the stem of his glass in a way that dried her throat in some inexplicable manner. 'If you're asking whether or not I usually date my employees, the answer is an emphatic "No."' He added, 'Besides, this isn't really a date.'

She flushed. 'No—no, I understand that.'

'But it will be next time.' It was said casually, almost thrown away, and, with that, the wine arrived, followed almost immediately by their first course choices, and Tarn, biting back an instinctive gasp of surprise, was left floundering, even wondering if she'd heard him correctly.

Because it was all happening too fast. And this was not part of the plan at all. He was not supposed to be in control. She was.

She tried to concentrate her whole attention on the *gnocchi* in its wonderful creamy sauce, but, in spite of herself, found that she was stealing covert glances at him under her lashes. No matter what her secret feelings might be, she could

not deny his attraction. Or this slow, almost in-
exorable build in her physical awareness of him.
His mouth—the way his smile lit his eyes, just as
Evie had said—his hands…

All of them things she had not allowed for. And
what she least wanted to deal with.

But, for now, there was chat. In any other circumstances, an easy, relaxed exchange of views
on books, music and the theatre. Perfectly normal
and acceptable. But, here and now, feeling more
like a journey through a minefield.

Don't be paranoid, she whispered silently.
*Where's the harm in his knowing you like
Margaret Atwood and John Le Carré? What
does it matter if you prefer Bach to Handel and
Mozart to both of them? Is it a state secret that
your favourite Shakespeare play is Much Ado
about Nothing?*

*For heaven's sake, relax. You needed to engage
his interest. You've succeeded beyond your wild-
est dreams. So capitalise on it.*

The *saltimbocca* was served, delicate veal esca-
lopes wrapped round *prosciutto* and sage leaves,
accompanied by green beans and lightly sautéed
potatoes. The white wine, fragrant as a flower,
was poured.

Caz raised his glass. 'I should propose a toast,'

he said. '"To us" seems slightly presumptuous at this stage, so let's drink to the health of your patient instead, and hope for a complete recovery.'

Her hand jerked, and a few droplets of wine splashed on to her shirt as she stared at him.

She said huskily, 'What do you mean?'

His brows lifted in faint surprise. 'I was told you were back in London because of a family illness. Did Rob Wellington get it wrong?'

'No, he's perfectly correct,' she said. She drew a deep breath. Forced a smile. 'I—I suppose I didn't expect him to pass it on.'

'He feels you'll become a potentially valuable member of the workforce, and is worried we'll lose you.' He paused. 'I imagine you'll be planning to return to the States at some point—when there's no longer any cause for concern.'

'Why, yes,' she said. 'But it probably won't be any time soon. Progress is steady but slow, I'm afraid.'

'Is it a close relative who's sick?'

'My cousin.' She met his gaze calmly. 'She hasn't anyone else.' After all, Aunt Hazel was out of the equation for the foreseeable future, so it was almost the truth and easier to remember than an outright lie.

'I'm sorry,' he said. 'It must be very worrying for you.'

'Well, yes, it was at first,' Tarn said. *And how dare you say you're sorry when you don't mean it—utter some meaningless, clichéd regret when it's all your fault that it ever happened.*

She swallowed back the words—the accusations that she wanted to scream at him. Introduced a bright note into her voice. 'But I hope she's over the worst of it now.'

That was good, she thought. That suggested an eventual happy outcome on the horizon. And not a hint of breakdown, or isolation, or the kind of secrets that would lead to destruction.

At the same time, she didn't want to answer any more questions in case the answers became too revealing, so she decided to drag the conversation back to less personal topics.

She looked down at her plate. 'You were right about the veal,' she added lightly. 'It's delicious— absolutely marvellous.'

'So you'd risk having dinner with me again?'

Oh, God, out of the frying pan straight into the fire...

She drank some of her wine, letting it blossom in her mouth, while she considered what to say.

'I don't think that would be altogether appropriate.' She permitted herself a rueful shrug.

'Ah,' he said. 'For the reasons already stated?'

'Of course.'

'And not because you find me physically repugnant?'

She leaned back in her chair. 'Now you're laughing at me.'

'Not really,' he said. 'Simply trying to establish quite an important point. Well?'

She hesitated. Sent him a defensive look. 'You don't make things easy, do you?'

'Perhaps not,' he said softly. 'Maybe because I prefer to aim for—ultimately and mutually rewarding.'

The words seemed to shiver along her nerve-endings as if her senses were suddenly awakening to undreamed-of possibilities. Her skin was warming as though it had been brought alive by the stroke of a hand. Her nipples were hardening, aching, inside the lace confines of her bra. And while the immediacy of her response might be shocking, it was, to a certain extent, understandable.

Because instinct told her that Caz Brandon was not simply suggesting the likelihood of sensual delight, but offering it to her as a certainty.

An overwhelming prospect for someone of her ludicrously limited experience, she thought, and stopped right there, suppressing a gasp.

Oh, dear God, what was she doing to herself? Was she going completely crazy? Because she knew perfectly well that whatever he might be promising was never going to be fulfilled.

Evie, Evie, she whispered under her breath. *If this is how he came on to you, no wonder you simply fell into his hands. He could make anyone believe anything.*

Yet she was in no real danger, she reminded herself emphatically. Not when she could visualise her foster sister lying in that bed, in that clinical room, her slender body reduced to painful thinness, and her once-pretty face a haggard mask of unhappiness. That was the image that would armour her against succumbing to the wiles of the man confronting her across the candle-lit table.

He said, 'I was always told that silence means consent. But with you I need assurance. Does it?'

She pulled herself together, and met his gaze directly. She said in a low voice, 'How can I possibly answer you? We hardly know each other.'

'How strange that you should think so,' he said. 'Because I felt a kind of instant recognition, and thought you were conscious of it too. As if it was inevitable I would look up some evening and find you standing on the other side of the room.'

He was actually shaking his head. 'It's never happened to me before. If I'm to be candid, I didn't particularly expect it or want it.' His smile was brief almost harsh. 'You're an extra complication, Tarn Desmond, in an already crowded existence.'

'So I believe.' The swift, taut reply was framed before she could stop herself. Fool, she castigated herself silently. Imbecile. Although his private life was hardly a state secret. That there were pictures of him with various glamorous companions all over the Internet. With one exception...

His slow answering grin mingled amusement with pleasure.

'So you've been checking up on me,' he said. 'That's encouraging.'

'Professional interest,' she told him coolly. 'I like to know the calibre of the people I work for.'

His former words were still ringing in her head. Presumably this was his tried and tested line, she thought, the sheer arrogance of the man catching her by the throat.

It should have made her furious—hardened her resolve, but instead she felt momentarily flurried—almost bewildered.

'And yet you took Philip Hanson at face value,' he said. 'Why was that?'

'A momentary glitch,' she said after a swift, startled silence. She'd almost forgotten that particular fiction. 'He was very convincing.'

'He must have been.' His mouth twisted. 'You'd certainly pulled out the stops when you were dressing that evening, and all for someone you hardly knew. Was that wise?'

'I didn't dress for him,' Tarn defended. 'I wanted to make an impression at the party.'

'Then you certainly succeeded,' Caz told her. He frowned. 'Yet I still wonder why he steered you towards us. I'm not complaining you understand, just—slightly puzzled.' He paused. 'You haven't tried to track him down since?'

She shrugged. 'I wouldn't know where to start. I suppose I really do have to treat it as a stupid, unkind joke.'

'If so, it was one that signally misfired,' Caz returned drily. 'We should both be grateful to him.'

'Both of us?' Her brows lifted. 'I rather think all the gratitude's on my side. Because I must also thank the girl who's having a baby, and created a vacancy for me, however temporary.'

'This is beginning to sound like an Oscars ceremony,' he said. 'In a minute, you'll be blessing your parents for having you.'

Perhaps, she thought. If I'd ever known them. If they hadn't left me alone in the world, dependant on strangers.

Aloud, she said, 'And what's so wrong about that?'

'Nothing,' he said. 'Except it's a task you should really leave to me.'

Tarn looked away. She said, 'If all this is another joke, can we end it here and now, please. I think it's gone quite far enough.'

'This is a beginning,' Caz told her quietly. 'Not a closing. But I can see I'm going to have to work damned hard to prove to you that I'm serious.'

And with that, the waiters appeared to clear their plates, and produce dessert menus, giving Tarn a much-needed breathing space as she contemplated what to say next. How to react.

Tricky, when all she really wanted to do was empty the remains of that expensive wine over his head, call him a treacherous, unfeeling bastard and storm out.

But that would only provide her with a momentary satisfaction. While he could laugh off his brief humiliation as a lovers' tiff, and every man in the restaurant would be on his side.

And what she wanted—required—was for him to experience the kind of pain that he'd inflicted on Evie.

And it will happen, she vowed inwardly. I'll make it happen.

'Tell me something,' he said, when the *panna cotta* with its red berry *coulis* had been ordered for them both. 'Is there someone in New York? Someone you plan to go back to?'

'Why do you ask?' She drank some more wine.

'Because I need to know what I'm up against. If it's just the office hierarchy thing that's making you so elusive, or if there's something or someone else.'

Or maybe I'm just trying to demonstrate that you're not Mr Irresistible, she told him silently. On the other hand, it would be stupid to let you think I'm totally uninterested and alienate you completely. So it's time to tug on the thread a little.

She met his gaze squarely. 'There's no-one,' she said. 'Not any more.'

This time it was the whole truth. Howard had reacted badly to the news that she would not be accompanying him to the Keys. And her subsequent explanation had left him not merely unmoved, but getting angrier by the moment.

'Everything you've ever told me about this Evie

says she's a total flake,' he'd finally thrown at her.
'You're crazy to get involved in her problems.
I had a lot riding on this trip, Tarn, and you've
just—blown it out of the water. And why?' His
voice had risen and people at adjoining tables had
glanced at them curiously. 'Because your sister's
boyfriend's dumped her? Big deal. What about
you—dumping on me? And what the hell do I
say to Jim and Rosemary?'

He'd finished his drink and left, leaving her to
pick up the check. Nor, she thought, could she really blame him.

She'd gauged when he'd be back from the Keys
and rung him. It was almost certainly over between them, such as it had been, but, all the same,
she didn't want to part bad friends. However, her
call had gone straight to voicemail, and not been
returned. So that episode in her life was definitely
in the past, and she only wished she could feel
more regret. Especially as he was probably the
closest she'd ever been to commitment.

But there was no point in thinking like that. One
day, when all this was over, she'd find someone.
Or maybe they'd find her. Wasn't that how it was
meant to be?

But before that could happen, she had a part to
play. Retribution to exact.

Caz said quite gently, 'I hope the parting wasn't too painful.'

She shrugged. 'Not very—especially when compared with other people's experiences.' She gave him a half-smile. 'I think I probably had a lucky escape.'

'Then I'll have to make sure that you'll continue to think so.'

There was a note in his voice which was almost a caress, and Tarn felt her skin shiver again in unwelcome response.

'And what about you? How have you managed to avoid serious involvement?' She spoke lightly, but she was stepping on to dangerous ground and she knew it, as her clasped fingers tightened painfully in her lap.

'It's never been a deliberate thing,' he said, after a pause. 'Until a year or so ago, hauling the company back from the brink occupied most of my time and energy. When the money men finally stopped scowling, I decided I could take life a little more easily. But that was all.

'Because I never pretended to the girls I dated that I was looking for any kind of permanent relationship. And most of them were looking for fun rather than commitment too, so we generally managed to reach a consensus that suited us both.'

She said, 'But there must have been some who hoped you would offer more.'

His mouth tightened, and he looked past her, his eyes suddenly remote. 'If so,' he said. 'That would be their problem, not mine.'

And one of those problems is locked away in a private hospital that's more like a prison, you unutterable bastard...

She said quietly, 'I shall consider myself warned.'

'That isn't what I meant, and you know it.' His tone was almost fierce. 'Give me the chance and I'll prove it to you. And whatever happened in the past is over—for both of us.'

The desserts appeared, and Tarn forced herself to eat the rich, creamy concoction with its sharp fruit counterpart with every sign of appreciation.

So where did the expensive diamond ring he'd given Evie feature in this no-commitment scenario? she asked herself. Or was that how he paid his women for services rendered?

She remembered a story she'd heard when she was a child about a girl finding the man she was to marry was another Bluebeard and exposing his guilt by flinging the severed and bejewelled ring finger of one of his victims on the table in front of him at their betrothal banquet.

If she could find Evie's ring, she thought, throw-

ing it at him in some public place would make a
splendid denouement for the moment when he
finally learned the truth about her. When he discovered it was his turn to be deceived and callously dumped.

And now, she thought, steeling herself, it's time
to proceed to the next stage.

So when coffee was offered, she declined, with
an anxious glance at her watch.

'My flatmate will be wondering where I am.'

'You're not living at your cousin's place?'

'It's minute,' she said. 'My stuff would fill
it, and I don't want her to come home and feel
squeezed out, so I've moved in temporarily with
a friend.'

'While you look for a place of your own?' Caz
asked as he dealt with the bill.

'Perhaps. I haven't decided yet.' She picked up
her bag. 'However—thank you for a wonderful
meal. You've been—' she hesitated '—very kind.'

'And it's equally kind of you to say so.' There
was a touch of wryness in his tone. 'My driver
will be coming to pick me up in a few minutes.
May I add to my good works and offer you a lift?'

'I think you've done enough,' she said. 'At least
for one evening.'

The hazel eyes danced. 'Is that a hint that there may be another in the offing?'

'It's a promise to think about it,' Tarn said sedately. 'Nothing more.'

'Then I shall simply have to hope for the best.'

They were outside now, and he hailed a cruising taxi for her.

She gave the driver the address, burningly conscious that Caz was standing right beside her. Would he try to kiss her? She couldn't be sure.

But he merely opened the cab door and held it for her to climb in.

'That's dangerous thinking.' As she prepared to do so, she managed an impish smile. 'I might be the worst thing that's ever happened to you.'

He said softly, 'I'll take that risk.'

He handed the driver some money and stood back. As the cab sped off, Tarn wondered if he was watching, but nothing in the world could have persuaded her to turn and look.

You think the past is over? she whispered under her breath. *Oh, no, Mr Brandon, it's right here waiting for you. And I'm your unexpected nightmare.*

CHAPTER FOUR

'YOU had dinner with him?' Della stared at her, open-mouthed. 'With the Demon King? How—and why?'

Tarn shrugged. 'I was working late, he came back for his briefcase and we met. It was just—happenstance.'

'If one can believe in such a thing,' Della said with a touch of grimness. 'So tell me about it.'

'He took me to a wonderful restaurant, great food, fabulous wine—and he came on to me.'

'In what way?' Della leaned against the kitchen worktop. 'The direct approach? "My place or yours?"'

'Far from it.' Tarn poured herself some coffee, and refilled Della's beaker. 'A well-practised speech full of love, romance and "the first time I saw you" stuff.' She gave a contemptuous snort. 'My God, even if Evie wasn't involved, I'd want to see him get his comeuppance. It shows how little respect he has for women. He must think

I'm a total idiot if he expects me to fall for that
old routine.'

Della's eyes widened. 'So, your life has been
punctuated by men laying their lives at your feet,
is that what you're saying?'

'No, of course not.' Tarn frowned. 'But—oh,
hell, you know what I mean.' She paused, then
added casually, 'Besides, the entire world knows
he's seeing Ginny Fraser from the "Up to the
Minute" show.'

'Seeing each other's brains out, by all accounts,'
Della agreed cordially. 'Therefore you haughtily
rejected his unwanted advances and swept off into
the night. Right?'

Tarn shifted uncomfortably. 'Not exactly.'

'What then?'

'He asked if he could have dinner with me again,
and, naturally, I said I'd think about it.'

'Well, naturally,' Della echoed ironically. There
was a silence, then she sighed. 'Tell me something, Tarn. If Evie didn't feature in this scenario,
and you'd simply met Caz Brandon at a party
and you'd spent time together, and he'd suggested
another meeting, would you have said "Yes" to
him?'

'No,' Tarn said passionately. 'Never in a million

years. Because I don't go for arrogant, all con-
quering men.'

'Hmm,' said Della. 'Some might say you're
being a trifle picky, but that's your choice.' She
paused again. 'However, I've always had a bad
feeling about this scheme of yours, and, somehow,
it's getting worse all the time. So—if you do go
out with him again—what then?'

'Nothing,' said Tarn. 'Not next time, the time
after that, or any time at all. I give him enough
encouragement to keep him interested, but he
stays strictly at arms' length until he's actually
desperate. And then I choose the time and place
to tell him that he's an uncaring swine and why I
wouldn't have him if he came gift-wrapped.'

'But do you really think he'll care—given that
he's apparently one of the major bastards of the
western world? Maybe he'll just shrug and walk
away.'

'That would depend on how many other people are around at the time. And mud sticks. He'll
find himself being talked about in ways he won't
like. So I hit him twice—firstly in his belief he's
sexually irresistible. Secondly in his self image
as the great publishing tycoon. He'll know I've
been laughing at him all the time, and he's going
to have to live with that for the rest of his life.'

'Sweet suffering saints,' said Della. She shook her head wonderingly. 'You really intend to go to those lengths? A public denunciation?'

'Of course,' Tarn said defiantly. 'Ever since I re-read Evie's letters, and saw how much in love she'd been with him. When I realised exactly what he'd done. How appallingly he'd treated her.'

'And do you also realise how easily you could come unstuck?' Della demanded roundly. 'He's not a boy but an experienced and very attractive man, so you may not find him as easy to distance as you think. And when he finds he's been made a fool of, things could get even trickier.'

Tarn shrugged. 'It's a risk worth taking. Besides, as I've told you, he doesn't appeal to me.'

There was a loaded silence, then Della said quietly, 'Honey, it's still not too late to ditch the plan and run.'

'Don't tell me you're concerned for him!'

'I'm concerned for you. Tarn—this is all so out of character. You're not the vengeful type.'

'I'm learning to be.'

'Then stop now, while you can, before any real damage is done, to you or him. Hand in your notice, head back to the States, or, if you feel like a change, find a place to rent in Europe and resume real life.

'Evie may have had a rough time, but she might get over it much more easily if you're not there dispensing sympathy and muttering vengeance.'

'You didn't see her.' Tarn spread her hands. 'See the terrible state she was in—and all down to that utter bastard.'

'But you can't spend your future protecting Evie from unsuitable men,' Della objected. 'Or dealing with the consequences if she gets drawn in. She's got to learn to look after herself—to discriminate between the decent guys and the rats.'

'She hasn't anyone else.' *The same words she'd used earlier to Caz Brandon.*

'That is so not true,' Della said firmly. 'Actually, if you did but know it, she does have a mother. Who rang up earlier, as it happens, in a state over Evie's flat. It seems the landlord wants it cleared out if she's not coming back, and there's some rent owing too. Apparently La Mère Griffiths is passing up this belated but golden opportunity to take on some of the responsibility for her daughter and wants you to sort it out instead. So no surprises there.'

'It's not altogether her fault,' Tarn said, with a faint sigh. 'Uncle Frank took care of everything. Until he died, I don't think she'd ever had to pay a bill or speak to a bank.'

'And he passed the over-protective mantle on to you.' Della nodded. 'Well, that makes a kind of sense.'

'And Caz Brandon has got to learn that having power and money does not absolve you from all sense of decency,' Tarn added fiercely. 'Before he destroys some other poor girl's life.'

'Then I just hope you're not numbering Ginny Fraser among his unfortunate victims.' Della finished her coffee and rinsed the beaker. 'In the ruthless ambition stakes, she could probably leave him standing.' She moved to the door. 'Sweet dreams, honey, and tomorrow, please wake up cured. Or even slightly more sane would do.'

But if anything Tarn only felt more determined when she opened unwilling eyes in response to the radio alarm next morning. She'd had a restless night, interspersed with brief, uneasy dreams. Things she preferred not to remember in the light of day.

She paused while cleaning her teeth and studied herself in the bathroom mirror. There were shadows under her eyes, and her cheekbones looked stark in their prominence. Not really the kind of look to appeal to a would-be seducer.

I need to relax, she thought. Smile more, or

he could change his mind and walk away. And I can't let that happen, because, whatever Della may think, he's asked for everything that's coming to him.

'Congratulations,' was Lisa's greeting as Tarn entered the All Your Own editorial suite. She shook her head. 'You're the original dark horse, my girl, just full of surprises and succeeding where others could only fail. I can hardly believe it.'

My God, Tarn thought shakily. Someone must have seen me with him last night, and word's got round already. This was not what I'd planned at all. The opposite, in fact.

She tried to speak steadily. 'What do you mean?'

'I mean, my pet, that you seem to have waved some kind of magic wand and turned dear Annetta into a writer.' Lisa picked up the draft script and waved it like a flag. 'This can actually go into the schedules. In fact, I'm debating whether we should build on this and do a whole series of celeb stories, that is if you're prepared to pick up the slack and spin the straw into gold.'

'Chameleon' on a small scale, Tarn thought ironically. This was getting rather too close to reality. And why hadn't she seen it coming?

She marshalled a smile. 'That sounds a marvellous idea. But do you think the accountants will wear it?'

'They will if Caz tells them to.' Lisa's expression was catlike. 'And maybe we can offer him a sweetener by including Ginny Fraser on the list.'

Pain, sudden and astonishing, twisted inside Tarn like a sharpened knife. But somehow she let her smile widen. Become conspiratorial. 'Then let's go for it. What have we got to lose?'

Lisa nodded. 'I'll send a proposal up to him as soon as he gets back.'

'Oh.' Tarn paused on her way back to her desk. She kept her tone casual. 'Is he away somewhere?'

'Paris, Madrid, then Rome,' said Lisa. 'One of his usual rounds.'

So much for forward planning, thought Tarn wryly. She'd dressed that morning in a brief black skirt that showed off her slim legs, teaming it with a scoop-necked white top that might be deemed by the purists as a fraction too low for office wear, and she'd left her hair loose.

She'd been so sure he'd waste no time in finding an excuse for their paths to cross again, or press for an answer to his invitation in some other way. Had been bracing herself, in fact, for a summons. So, why hadn't he mentioned his trip the previous evening?

Because he didn't have to, she told herself, biting her lip as she stared at her computer screen. Because last night he acted on an impulse which he probably regretted just as quickly, and this is the cooling-off period. When he returns, he'll have other things on his mind and he can allow the whole thing to slide quietly into oblivion.

Which takes me right back to square one.

She bit her lip, and switched on her computer. She'd worry about that later when she'd finished work. Now she needed to concentrate.

But when the working day was over, there was Aunt Hazel to attend to. She'd phoned twice, the first time to make sure Della had passed on her message—'I thought she seemed very casual'— and the second to remind Tarn she'd need to call round and pick up Evie's key and the address.

When Tarn arrived at Wilmont Road, she found her foster mother peevish.

'I thought you were never going to get here.' She picked up an envelope. 'The rent money's in here. Six hundred pounds in cash, as he insisted.' She pursed her lips. 'How very unreasonable people can be, harassing me like this when he must know I'm half out of my mind with worry. But at least it means my girl will be coming back here to her own home when she's better.'

'I suppose he's entitled to be paid,' Tarn said mildly. 'And to look for another tenant.'

'Oh, poor Evie.' Mrs Griffiths shook her head, tearfully. 'She should never have gone to live in that flat. I knew no good would come of it.'

And this time, Tarn could only agree.

Evie had said that Caz had arranged for the move, so Tarn expected her cab to drop her at some smart apartment block. Instead she found herself outside a tall house in a busy street filled with identical buildings, many of which had clearly seen better days. She walked over chipped paving stones past a row of over-stuffed wheelie bins, wondering if Aunt Hazel had sent her to the wrong place.

But one of the keys fitted the front door, and she walked into a narrow hall. There was only one door clearly leading to the ground floor flat, where Mrs Griffiths had said the landlord lived, and most of the remaining space was occupied by a bicycle leaning against one wall, and a narrow side table littered with junk mail pushed against the other.

If he owns the place why doesn't he clear it up a little, thought Tarn pressing the bell. She rang twice and waited, but there was no reply, so she mounted the uncarpeted stairs to the next floor and Flat Two.

She unlocked the door with faint trepidation, wondering what she would find, but the interior turned out to be a distinct improvement. The small square hall was flooded with light from a big window overlooking some overgrown but attractive back gardens.

The bedroom, she saw, was directly opposite the entrance, its half-open door revealing an unmade bed and the kind of serious clutter a hurricane might leave in its wake.

Tarn wondered, with a faint shiver, if that was where Evie had been found, and hastily turned her attention to the comfortably sized living area with its galley kitchen, accessed by three shallow steps down from the hall.

The carpet and furnishings were not new but they looked clean and in reasonable nick. She'd seen very much worse in her travels.

But this was still far from the kind of love nest that she would ever have envisaged for Caz Brandon. Evie must have been totally blinded by passion not to realise she was being offered a pretty third-rate set-up.

But she wasn't here to speculate, she reminded herself, or even to build up her resentment and bitterness towards Caz, although this visit was simply confirming everything she'd thought about him. Her job was to clear out Evie's stuff.

There was an inventory pinned to the galley notice board, which demonstrated that Evie had been content to stick with what was provided and make no individual additions to the utensils, or the china, glassware and cutlery either. But then cooking had never been a big thing to Evie.

Nor had the living space benefited from her attention. Every cushion, picture, and sparse selection of ornaments was also listed.

So Tarn was forced to face the bedroom, and the cramped en-suite shower room which opened off it.

It was unlikely Evie would wish any reminders of the room, she thought as she stripped the bed, and bundled the bedding into a plastic sack, before filling a hold-all with Evie's clothes and shoes. Although, from a psychological point of view, she realised, it might be better to get rid of all of them too, and start again from scratch.

Emptying the wardrobe didn't take much doing. For a girl who'd been living the high life with a millionaire boyfriend, Evie didn't seem to have a lot of clothes, and what there was didn't rate highly on glamour, thought Tarn, wondering what had happened to the chiffon and lace wedding dress as she emptied the small tallboy.

The drawer in the bedside cabinet would only open fractionally, and she realised something was stuck there. After a brief struggle and a bruised knuckle or two, she managed to release it and extract the culprit, which turned out to be a square, leather-bound book.

Of course, she thought. It's Evie's diary. I should have known. And she must be missing it. In the past, she probably hasn't missed a day without writing in it. I wonder if they'd let her have it at The Refuge. It might be therapeutic for her.

She slipped it into her shoulder bag, then returned to the drawer. Small wonder it had stuck, she thought, discovering an envelope bulging with paperwork which she decided to take with her too, in case there was something incriminating about Caz among its contents. And under the envelope, she found a scrapbook. One glance told her that every single newspaper cutting and photograph that filled its pages featured Caz. And maybe all this material explained why there were no actual framed photographs of him in the flat. Unless, of course, Evie had never been given such a keepsake.

Whatever, this will not be going with me, she

told herself grimly, adding the scrapbook to the bin bag.

Then, as she felt further towards the back of the drawer, she encountered something else—a small square jeweller's box covered in black velvet.

She opened it and gasped aloud at the blaze of the stones that glittered like ice-blue fire in Evie's engagement ring.

My God, she muttered under her breath. No wonder she believed every rotten lie he told her. Each of them must have cost an entire carat. But why on earth did he bother? Unless it had always been intended as a kiss-off payment, she thought, wincing.

She closed the box with a snap, and dropped that into her shoulder bag too.

The shower room was easily cleared, all the half-used toiletries swept into the bin bag along with the remains of the packs of painkillers, in-digestion tablets and Evie's contraceptive pills, which were all that the small medicine cabinet over the washbasin contained.

No sign of the sleeping tablets Evie had used for her overdose.

She fastened the tie handles on the plastic sack and carried it back into the bedroom, where she stopped, gasping.

A man was standing in the doorway, thin and barely above medium height with very pale blond hair and light blue eyes, dressed in a grey suit with a faint silky sheen that whispered expensive.

He said softly, 'Exactly who are you? And what are you doing here?'

This, thought Tarn, recovering her breath, must be the troublesome landlord.

She said crisply, 'Quite obviously I'm removing Miss Griffiths' possessions as requested. But perhaps it's a trick question.' She paused. 'And I have your money.'

The fair brows lifted. 'Do you indeed? Well, that is good news.' He glanced around. 'Do I take it that Evie will not be returning?'

Tarn stared at him. 'But you know that already. You told her mother you wanted to re-let the place.'

'Ah.' The thin mouth stretched into a smile. 'I think there's a slight misunderstanding here. My name is Roy Clayton and I actually live upstairs, another of Bernie the Bloodsucker's hapless tenants. I heard someone moving around down here, came to investigate and found the door unlocked.'

'But you didn't ring the bell,' said Tarn.

'Er—no. Evie and I weren't on such formal terms.' He paused. 'And you are?'

'Her sister.'

'What a charming surprise. I didn't know she had one.' His smile widened a little. 'Such a dreadful thing to have happened. You must all be devastated. I was the one who found her, you know, and called the ambulance.'

'No,' Tarn said. 'I didn't know that.'

'So is she fully on the road to recovery? And can she have visitors, wherever she happens to be?'

'She's making satisfactory progress,' Tarn returned. 'But she's not up to seeing people yet.'

'What a pity.' He glanced round the room again, his gaze lingering on the suitcase and the empty bedside cabinet, while Tarn took a quick look at her shoulder bag beside the chest of drawers, checking that it hadn't been disturbed because Evie's ring was in there.

He added, 'Bernie should have told me that she wasn't coming back. I could have saved you a journey and a job, and cleared the place for you.'

'That's kind of you,' Tarn said untruthfully. 'But it's probably a task better suited to her family.'

'I'm sure you're right.' The curiously pale eyes rested on her. 'You mentioned something about money?'

She looked back at him, bewilderment mixing

with her unease. 'Yes—but I thought you were the landlord wanting his rent.'

'Oh, dear, another disappointment,' he said lightly.

'You mean Evie owed you too?' She drew a dismayed breath, bracing herself. 'If you'll tell me what it was for and how much, perhaps something could be arranged.'

'Oh, I couldn't possibly put you to so much trouble,' he said. 'And it's really quite a trivial matter. Besides, I'm sure Evie and I will be running into each other again. One of these days. When she's better.'

He paused again. 'Now I'll leave you to your toil. Do tell Evie next time you see her that I was asking about her. You won't forget, will you?' Another swift smile, and he was gone.

Tarn stayed where she was, uncomfortably aware that her breathing had quickened, and the plastic sack in her hand seemed suddenly to be weighing a ton.

Oh, pull yourself together, she told herself sharply. He's just a concerned guy from upstairs. You're letting this whole Caz Brandon thing knock you sideways, make you imagine every man you come across is a potential threat.

On the other hand, as she went downstairs, she

found the genuine article waiting for her, bald and tattooed in a football shirt and denim cut-offs.

'Bernie Smith.' He gave her a hard look. 'You're not the woman I talked to.'

'No, that was Miss Griffiths' mother.'

He grunted. 'Got the rent?'

Tarn handed over the envelope and watched him count it.

'Seems to be all there,' he said. 'Lucky I don't charge for having the place cleaned. And the inconvenience—paramedics and police swarming all over. Gives a place a bad name.'

'Difficult to see how,' Tarn said, giving the hallway a disparaging look before dropping the keys into his hand.

'No need to be so high and mighty,' he called after her, as she left. 'And I'll be checking that inventory, no danger.'

But I shall not, Tarn thought, as she hailed a cab, be mentioning any of this to Aunt Hazel.

'Are you sure you won't come to Molly's birthday bash tonight?' asked Della. 'She said you'd be more than welcome.'

Tarn shook her head. 'I'm going to have a long bath, wash my hair, and go through the stuff in the envelope yet again, in case I'm still missing something.'

'Like a proposal of marriage from Caz Brandon in writing?' Della wrinkled her nose. 'You can't sue for breach of promise any longer.'

Tarn sighed. 'I wasn't thinking of that. I'm just trying to make sense of it all. To correlate the weird flat with that amazing ring, the chainstore clothing with the millionaire lifestyle.'

'A noble ambition,' said Della. 'And I'm sure Evie would do just as much for you.'

Tarn bit her lip. 'But you must admit it's strange.'

'Strange is not the word. And at the risk of turning into Cassandra whose warnings were also ignored, I say again that you should drop the entire mess, and get back to your own life.' She gave Tarn a minatory glance. 'A decision that Mr Brandon may also have made.'

'Apparently he was bankrolling her,' Tarn said unhappily. 'There were some nasty letters from the bank and a credit card company in the envelope, but a week later she's writing in her diary that she no longer has any money worries, "thanks to C."'

'Exactly,' said Della. 'He must have realised she was a total flake, especially where money was

concerned, and that he'd be lucky if she didn't
bankrupt him.'

'But he was going to marry her,' Tarn argued.
'Why didn't he sit down and talk to her if there
was a problem? Try to work things out?'

Della shrugged. 'Maybe he did, and found it
was stony ground.'

'There's also a load of stuff about the MacNaughton
Company,' Tarn said, producing a sheaf of papers.
'Whoever they are.'

'Now there I can help,' said Della. 'They're a
cleaning firm, incredibly high-powered, lethally
expensive, and very discreet, exclusively employed by the mega-rich and famous. They appear like good elves, perform their wonders and
vanish.' She frowned. 'But from what you've
said, Evie's flat wouldn't be their usual stamping
ground, even if she could afford them.'

'I gather from her diary that Caz Brandon fixed
her up with them too,' Tarn said wearily. 'Though
there wasn't much sign that professional cleaners
had ever been there.'

Della was silent for a moment. 'The guy upstairs—was he attractive?'

'He gave me the creeps.'

'But you, honey, are not Evie. Could she have

been two-timing her fiancé with the neighbourhood watch, do you suppose?'

'Never in this world,' Tarn said with emphasis.
'No-one who was seeing Caz Brandon would give
Roy Clayton a second glance.'

'Is that a fact?' Della said affably. 'How very
interesting that you should think so.'

She picked up her bag and walked to the door.
'If you get tired of your mysteries, Sherlock, we'll
all be at the Sunset Bar,' she threw over her shoulder as she left.

An hour later, Tarn was wishing she'd taken
up the offer. Wrapped in a towelling robe, her
hair curling damply on her shoulders, she was en-
sconced in a corner of the sofa, re-reading Evie's
diary and getting more depressed by the minute.

The contrast between the almost hysterical happiness at the beginning of her relationship with
Caz and the agonised descent into despair when
it ended was almost too painful to contemplate.

'What can I do? I can't go on?' were words repeated over and over again. But Tarn had an odd
sense from the later entries that Evie was not just
wretched, but frightened too, because *'What will
happen to me? Where will I go?'* also cropped up
with alarming frequency.

What did he do to her? she thought.

She reached for the beaker of coffee she'd made earlier, realising with a grimace that it was now cold. She closed the diary, put it on the floor with the envelope, and rose to go to the kitchen.

She was waiting for the kettle to boil when the door bell sounded.

Della must have forgotten her key again, she thought, although it seemed rather early for the birthday celebrations to have ended.

A teasing remark already forming in her mind, she walked to the front door and threw it open.

And stood, as if turned to stone, as she stared at her caller.

'Good evening,' said Caz Brandon, and he smiled at her.

CHAPTER FIVE

SILENCE stretched between them, threatening to become endless as shock held her motionless. Speechless. Yet she had to do something…

'You.' Her mouth was dry. She hardly recognised her own voice. 'What are you doing here?'

His shrug was rueful. 'I'd hoped to take you to dinner, but my flight was delayed, so my guess is you've already eaten.'

He paused, the cool hazel gaze sweeping over her. His expression did not change, but Tarn's instincts told her that he knew perfectly well that she was naked under the towelling robe. She had to resist an impulse to tighten her sash, and draw the lapels more closely to her throat.

He added, 'I seem to have called at an inopportune moment, so maybe a drink is out of the question too?'

She made no immediate response and his brows rose with faint mockery. 'Another loaded silence,' he remarked. 'I suppose I shall have to become accustomed to that.'

She went on staring at him. 'How did you find me?'

'Quite easily. Your contact details including your address are all logged at the office—as you must know.'

Of course she did, but she was playing for time, trying to pull her scattered wits together.

She said slowly, 'I'm not exactly geared up for going out. And we don't keep much in the way of alcohol.'

'I'd settle for coffee,' he suggested. 'I might even drink it here at the door, if you insist.' He went on softly, 'Although I promise I don't pounce, or, at least, not without a serious invitation.'

Her smile was brief and unwilling. 'I think it would probably be better if you came in.'

He followed her into the flat. 'You looked as if you'd seen a ghost,' he commented. 'Surely you were expecting me to make contact?'

'Not really.' She hunched a shoulder. 'Men often say things that they don't mean, or that appear less enticing the next day.'

'Then you must have been unlucky in your men friends.'

As she walked ahead of him into the sitting

room, the first thing she saw was Evie's diary lying on the carpet by the sofa.

Oh, God, she thought. Having been involved so closely with her, he'll recognise that as soon as he sees it.

She said with a kind of insane brightness, 'It's so untidy in here. I must apologise.'

She moved quickly, gathering it up under the cover of the envelope that lay beside it, and pushing them both on to a shelf in the bookcase.

Caz was glancing round. 'This is a pleasant room.'

Better than the place you found for Evie...

Aloud she said, 'Thank you. Won't you sit down?'

'I have been sitting,' he said. 'On a plane, and then in the car that picked me up at the airport. May I help with the coffee instead?'

She hesitated, then led the way to the kitchen. It was a comfortable size, but tonight it felt cramped, as if by the simple action of turning from the sink to the worktop and from the worktop to a cupboard, she would brush against him.

She was almost surprised to discover she'd managed to assemble the coffee beans, the grinder and the percolator without any physical contact with him whatsoever.

Yet it was the mental awareness of him that she found so disturbing. The consciousness that he was leaning against the doorframe silently observing her flustered preparations.

She said, holding up a bottle, 'I've also found some brandy, but I think it's what Della uses for cooking, so I can't vouch for it.'

He grinned. 'No point being snobs in an emergency. Where do you keep your glasses?'

'Top cupboard on your right.'

As she spooned the freshly ground coffee into the percolator and added boiling water, the aroma filled the air, replacing the faint, expensive hint of musk that she'd detected from the cologne he wore.

When she'd decided to let him in, it was with the fixed intention of provoking him into making a pass, and then reporting him to the police for sexual harassment.

But wiser counsels had soon prevailed. The fact that she'd admitted him when she was alone and only wearing a bathrobe would do her case no good at all, she admitted silently. Besides, he'd said he wouldn't pounce, so she would have to make all the running—another serious black mark against her.

And the fact that this was Della's flat, and her

friend totally disapproved of what she was doing stopped her in her tracks, at least for tonight, and warned her to think of something else.

'I'm hoping this might relax you,' Caz remarked, handing her a rounded crystal glass. 'You look like a kitten caught in headlights—as if you don't know which way to run. Am I really so scary?'

'No,' she said. 'No, of course not. It was just—such a surprise. Besides, I'm not really dressed for entertaining.'

If she'd expected some leering riposte, she was disappointed.

Caz frowned slightly. 'I should have telephoned ahead. Warned you I was calling round, or maybe made a date for a more convenient time.'

'Then why didn't you?'

'Considering the amount of twitch in the air, maybe I should reserve my reasons for another time too.'

'I have a better idea,' Tarn said. 'Why don't we just—start again.' She held out her hand. 'Good evening, Mr Brandon. What an unexpected pleasure.'

'Change Mr Brandon to Caz,' he said, the warm strong fingers closing round hers. 'And it will become an unmitigated pleasure.'

And I'm an unmitigated fool not to throw this

brandy over you here and now and scream what you've done to your face—tell you what a bastard—what a love rat you are. Although you wouldn't recognise or understand the word 'love.' And, anyway, you'd just shrug it off and walk away. Water off a duck's back. But some day soon, you'll be made to care...

She allowed her long lashes to sweep down in demure concealment, in case he read the truth in her eyes. 'Very well—Caz.'

'A moment I might have missed if I'd called in advance,' he said softly as he released her hand. He paused. 'So where's your flatmate this evening?'

'At a hen party. Someone's birthday.'

'You didn't want to go?'

She sent him a wry glance. 'I decided to settle for a quiet night in.'

'Which I've spoiled,' he said softly. 'However, your loss is my definite gain.'

She set a tray with cups and saucers, adding a jug of cream. Caz carried it into the sitting room, placing it on the small table in front of the sofa, and she followed with the percolator. She sat at one end of the sofa, and he occupied the other, stretching long legs in front of him.

'I like the shampoo you use,' he commented un-expectedly. 'Apple with a hint of vanilla.'

Tarn busied herself pouring coffee, leaning forward so that the swing of her hair could conceal the sudden warmth invading her face.

She said, 'You're—very perceptive.'

'I'm on a steep learning curve,' he said. 'Finding out about you.'

Her throat tightened nervously. Was he serious? Given his money and resources, if he really started to probe her background, what might he not unearth?

With a supreme effort, she kept her voice light, and her hand steady as she passed him his coffee. 'Well, that shouldn't take long. There isn't very much to discover.'

'On the contrary,' he said slowly. 'I suspect it could take a lifetime.'

He reached for his brandy glass and raised it. 'To us.'

She drank without repeating the toast. 'Isn't that still slightly presumptuous?'

'I hope not,' he said. 'I simply have to win you round to my way of thinking, that's all.'

Her breathing quickened. 'And if I can't be won?'

'Do you mean "can't"?' he asked. 'Or is it really "won't"?'

She moved a restive shoulder, replaced her glass on the table. 'Does it make a difference?'

'Not really,' he said. 'Whichever it is, you'll find I don't give up easily.'

There was a silence, then she said jerkily, 'Mr Brandon—Caz—this whole conversation is making me—uneasy. I think you should drink your coffee and leave.'

'I'm sorry if you feel uncomfortable with the situation.' He smiled at her. 'Now, I was thinking it was like a foretaste of the future. Me—back from business trip. You—with your hair just washed and no makeup. Both of us enjoying a nightcap together, knowing exactly how the evening will end, but content to wait. To savour every lovely moment.'

His gaze rested on her startled, parted lips then moved down to the flurried rise and fall of her breasts under the concealment of her robe.

He added with sudden roughness, 'For God's sake, Tarn. Don't you know that I'm nervous too. Have you forgotten what I said the other night?'

'No.' She paused. 'I—I haven't forgotten anything.'

'You said earlier that we'd start again, and that's what I'm asking for. A chance to prove to you that I mean what I say. And we'll go at your pace, not mine. That's a promise. When you come into my arms, it will be because you want to be there.'

His mouth twisted ruefully. 'Now relax, and drink your coffee, while we discuss our first real date.'

She gasped. 'You—really don't give up, do you?'

The hazel eyes glinted. 'You'd better believe it. And at the same time please understand that you have nothing to fear.'

No, she thought. You're the one who should be afraid.

She picked up her cup and drank, regarding him over its brim. 'So what do you have in mind for this date?'

'I thought we might go to the theatre. I have tickets for the opening of the new Lance Crichton play next Wednesday.'

Her brows lifted in disbelief. 'Heavens. Sprinkled with gold dust, I presume.'

'Almost,' he admitted. 'Are you interested?'

Her eyes danced. 'I think it's an offer I can't refuse. I saw Payment in Kind on Broadway and loved it.'

'Then I hope you'll tell him so. He got rather a mauling from some of the New York critics.'

She drew a breath. 'You mean I could meet him. Are you serious?'

'I'm sure it could be arranged.'

Tarn thought then shook her head regretfully. 'The play's quite tempting enough. I think that meeting Lance Crichton would turn my head completely.'

He smiled. 'You're not so easily overwhelmed.'

He drank the rest of his coffee and stood up.

'You're leaving?' The words were involuntary, and so, she realised with shock, was the note of disappointment in her voice.

'That was what you wanted a few minutes ago,' he said. 'If you remember. And I've got what I came for, so I'm quitting while I'm ahead. It's wiser and probably safer.' He paused. 'I'm sure I don't have to explain why.'

There was a sudden, odd tension in the room, making her skin tingle. Forcing her to catch her breath.

She made a business of scrambling to her feet. 'I—I'll see you out.'

'Fine,' he said equably. At the front door, he turned, looking down at her. 'If you asked me to stay, I would.' His voice was gentle, but the hazel eyes were asking questions for which, to her horror, she could find no answer. She looked back at him, mutely, pleadingly, and he nodded as if she'd spoken.

He said, 'Then I'll be in touch.' He took a strand of her hair and lifted it to his face. 'Apples and vanilla,' he said, and went.

Tarn leaned against the closed door, trembling. Dear God, she thought weakly, just for a moment there I was actually tempted. And he—*he*—let me off the hook. How shameful is that?

She washed up the cups and glasses, emptied the percolator and put everything away as if she'd spent the entire evening alone. She'd tell Della he'd been there—of course she would. But in her own time, which certainly wasn't tonight. She needed to get her head straight before she broached the subject.

In her room, she took off her robe and reached for her nightgown. But, on impulse, she let it drop to the floor, and slid into bed naked. The sheets were cool against her heated skin, the fabric a caress that tantalised, offering arousal without satisfaction.

Eyes wide, staring into the darkness, she moved restlessly, languorously, aware, deep within her, of a scald of yearning, as unwelcome as it was unfamiliar.

It was wrong to feel like this, she told herself feverishly. Wrong and hideously stupid. None of the men she'd met in the past had affected her in the same way. She'd enjoyed their company—even found it pleasant to be held—kissed—but never wanted more. Had not grieved when it ended.

At the same time, she'd wrinkled her nose derisively at the thought of Mr Right waiting patiently just off-stage.

Not that Caz Brandon would ever figure in that category for any woman, she added hastily. Unless of course it was Ginny Fraser. According to Della, they seemed well-matched. Another 'celebrity couple' in the making, smiling for the camera if not for each other.

And maybe, with the prospect of younger talent climbing the television ladder behind her, Ms Fraser would find a different kind of limelight sufficient compensation for her husband's practised womanising.

'They're welcome to each other,' Tarn whispered, turning on to her front and burying her face in the pillow. 'And, once this is over, I—I have my career to get back to.'

She tried to think of the next Chameleon project. A couple of tempting names had been dangled in front of her, but ghost-writing was a two way street. She would have to meet the subjects and talk to them. See if there was any kind of rapport which could develop into a platform of mutual trust and liking. A prospect that they would eventually open up to her completely, maybe even tell her things about themselves they hadn't guessed until then.

That was the best foundation, and while it was being established, either party could simply walk away. It happened, and sometimes she'd been sorry, but often relieved, scenting trouble ahead.

And now, suddenly, there was Lance Crichton, she thought. One of the most successful playwrights of his generation, yet a man who'd always shunned personal publicity, letting his work speak for itself.

But a man who undoubtedly had a story waiting to be told, if approached in the right way. Only she'd come across him at totally the wrong moment because she couldn't put out even the most discreet feeler without the risk of self-betrayal, she reminded herself, sighing. Until her work here was done, Chameleon had to remain another closely guarded secret.

And so did the way Caz Brandon could make her feel, she thought, and shivered.

'You found her diary?' repeated Professor Wainwright. 'May I see it, please?'

Tarn lifted her chin. 'I'd prefer to give it to Evie,'

she said quietly. 'She's always kept a diary from being a small child. Written in it every day. It was almost an obsession with her. I thought that having it back might help with her treatment.'

'I think I am the best judge of that, Miss Griffiths. Her case is a complex one. But the diary could be useful in other ways.' He held out his hand and Tarn hesitated.

'First, will you tell me something, Professor?'

'I cannot guarantee that. What do you want to know?'

'Her mother told me Evie had taken an overdose but I didn't find anything like that when I cleared her bathroom.'

'The police removed them. They are a very strong brand, known abroad as Tranquo, and not legally available for sale in this country. I gather their possible side-effects mean that they never will be so licensed. However, supplies of this drug, among other illicit forms of tranquillisers and stimulants, are regularly smuggled in for sale on black market networks.'

'Smuggled in? By whom?'

He shrugged. 'No-one is quite sure, but people who travel abroad a great deal on perfectly legitimate business, and therefore have not attracted the attention of the police or customs authorities are natural suspects.

'It is believed a lot of them are bought by the rich and famous initially for their own use, but then recommended to their friends and acquaintances. Because these drugs work, Miss Griffiths, in spite of their inherent and serious risks.' He paused. 'They also cost a great deal of money.'

'But Evie couldn't possibly have afforded anything like that,' Tarn protested. But Caz could, she thought. And he travels constantly. Could it be even remotely possible…

And found her mind closing against the thought.

'Well, that is something the police will wish to discuss with her when she has recovered sufficiently.'

Tarn stared at him. 'And you think that's all right, do you? Have you forgotten that Evie's not a criminal but a victim, driven to total desperation. And you must know why,' she added fiercely.

'Let us say a clearer picture is beginning to emerge.' He was unruffled. 'Now, may I have the diary?'

She surrendered it reluctantly, and watched him place it in a drawer of his desk.

She said, 'And may I go and see Evie?'

'Not today, Miss Griffiths. I regret that you've

had a wasted journey, but you are obviously upset, and it would be better to wait until you are calmer, and able to accept that what we do here is for your foster sister's ultimate good.'

She said, 'It may be a long time before I believe that.'

'Also I would prefer her not to know that we have her diary.' He paused. 'In future, perhaps you should telephone in advance and make sure your visit is convenient.'

'Yes,' she said, and rose from her chair. 'I shall. But let me assure you, Professor Wainwright, that nothing I've done or shall do for Evie will ever be wasted.'

The theatre bar was crowded, and alive with an excited buzz of conversation.

No doubt in anyone's mind that this was an occasion, thought Tarn drily as she waited for Caz to return with their interval drinks.

She'd felt as if she was strung up on wires as she'd dressed for the evening, choosing a plain black knee-length shift topped with a taffeta jacket striped in emerald and black. Her hair she'd fastened in a loose knot on top of her head, and she wore jet pendant ear-rings.

She looked, she thought judicially surveying

the finished article in the mirror, the image of a girl ready for a date with the most attractive man she'd ever met.

Not at all like someone who'd spent her recent days and nights wondering whether or not that same man might be a drug smuggler, and if she should take her suspicions to the authorities.

Eventually, she'd told herself wearily that she was crazy. Because being a womanising bastard and love rat did not make Caz Brandon a felon, much as she might wish it. And watching him get his just deserts did not necessarily mean jail.

Della had arranged to be elsewhere when Caz came to pick Tarn up.

'I don't trust myself not to scream, "She's out to get you, and not in a good way,"' she'd commented candidly.

Tarn said with difficulty, 'Dell—this isn't a joke.'

'No,' Della returned. 'In my view, it has all the makings of a tragedy. But that's your choice, honey.'

Now Tarn watched as he threaded his way through the general melee carrying her spritzer and his own Scotch and water. It took a while because he was constantly being halted to respond to greetings.

When he reached her side, Tarn said, 'Do you know everyone here tonight?'

'I know some, but I think a lot of the others believe they know me because of some past introduction.' His voice was rueful. 'If I had to remember their names, I'd be in difficulties.' He handed over her drink. 'Here's to Act Two.' He added softly, 'And I don't necessarily mean the play.'

'Ah, but I do.' She sent him a smile. Made it teasing. 'It's absolutely wonderful—especially as I haven't the faintest idea what to expect next.' She gave a faint whistle. 'Lance Crichton certainly knows how to put the audience's emotions through the wringer.'

Caz nodded. 'When Bateman made that last entrance, I thought the woman next to me was going to fly out of her seat.'

Tarn shuddered. 'I thought I might too. Although I've never heard of the actor who plays him. Proving how out of touch I am.'

'Rufus Blaine? He did a season at Stratford in minor roles, and people at the time were saying he was a star in the making. I think this Bateman portrayal has confirmed that.' He paused. 'Curious, isn't it, how the wicked usually get far more interesting roles than the good?'

Tarn shrugged. 'It sometimes seems the same in real life.'

'Isn't that a little cynical?'

'Probably.' She added lightly, 'Blame it on Bateman, and the shocks in store for us. I can hardly wait.'

'I'm delighted to hear it.' He hesitated. 'I was afraid you were regretting having accepted my invitation.'

'What made you think that?'

'You seemed very quiet when I came to pick you up.'

'Did I? Perhaps I find dating the boss a daunting prospect.'

'Has it occurred to you that I might be a little daunted too?'

'Frankly, no. Why should it?'

He said slowly, 'Because you're different. There's something guarded—unfathomable about you, Tarn.'

Why—because I'm not a pushover, falling enraptured at your feet?

'A woman of mystery?' she asked, brows lifted. 'Flattering but untrue, I'm afraid. What you see is what you get.'

'I think,' he said, 'that only time will convince me of that.'

At that moment, the bell sounded to signal their return to the auditorium.

And she really had been saved by it, Tarn thought, quashing a sudden bubble of hysteria as she walked sedately beside him back to the stalls. Because Caz Brandon was going to be no pushover either. He was far too perceptive for his own good—or hers.

Dear God, she thought, I shall have to be so careful. So terribly careful.

CHAPTER SIX

THE word 'Careful' sang in her brain as she sat tautly beside him in the back of the car on the journey back to the flat, waiting for him to lunge at her.

But it didn't happen. Instead he chatted about the play, the performances, and the almost unbearable tension of the final act. And when the car drew up outside the apartment block, he dismissed her protests and escorted her to her door.

He watched as she fumbled in her bag for her key. 'Am I going to be asked in again for coffee?'

'My flatmate will be asleep,' she said, hoping that a wide awake Della wouldn't suddenly appear to make a liar of her. 'I—I don't want to disturb her.' She added, 'Besides, your driver's waiting.'

'Of course,' Caz said softly, and smiled at her. 'And I can wait too.'

His gaze travelled down to her mouth and she knew that he was going to kiss her. Knew as well that there was no realistic way she could avoid this. That she must, at least, appear willing if her long term plan was to succeed.

Her whole body stirred as he bent towards her, and she felt the slow, painful thump of her heart-beat echo through every nerve-ending in her skin. *Careful...*

His hands were gentle on her shoulders, drawing her towards him, then his lips touched hers, brushing them swiftly, lightly in a caress as fleeting as an indrawn breath. A tease that promised but did not fulfil.

Then he released her and stood back, the hazel eyes quizzical as they scanned her flushed face.

'Goodnight,' he said quietly. 'Sleep well. I'll be in touch.' And went.

As she walked on unsteady legs into the sitting room, she heard from the street below the sound of the car pulling away, and stood rigidly, one clenched fist pressed against her breast.

Clever, she thought stormily. Oh, God, he was clever. But she could play games too. And somehow—however difficult it became—she intended to win.

Her interior warning to take care continued to hang over her, as the spring days brightened and lengthened, and Caz's campaign began in earnest.

However Tarn soon realised that he seemed to be keeping it deliberately low-key, not crowding her or bombarding her with demands for her company. Certainly not trying to sweep her off her feet as he'd done to Evie with high profile dates. But a couple of times a week, they dined together, or visited a cinema, or went to a concert or another play, the arrangements invariably made through text or voicemail on her mobile phone.

It would have been much easier, she thought unhappily, if she hadn't been forced to remind herself quite so often that the time spent with Caz was simply a means to an end and nothing more. Because that should have been a given.

She didn't want to enjoy any part of these occasions, much less allow the reasons for them to slip from her mind, even momentarily. It worried her too that when she was alone, she sometimes found that she was smiling to herself, remembering something he had said or done, and was then forced to pull herself together, thankful that, knowing what he really was, she had the power and the will to resist his charm.

And, as she told herself, it was a relief that was all she had to fight. Because one element of their relationship did not vary. Each time he brought her home, he kissed her briefly, grazing her mouth

with his, just once and departed. Leaving her restless and wondering what he was doing on the
other five days and nights when she didn't see
him, apart, of course, from the occasional glimpse
at work, generally on his way to or coming from
a meeting, and immersed in conversation.

Although Tarn was busy too. Lisa had been
given the go-ahead on the celebrity short story
series, and they were in contact with the 'A' list
they'd drawn up, so she had little time in office
hours to let her mind wander in his direction.

Which, as she reminded herself forcefully, was
all to the good.

What was not so good was the realisation that
she was actually enjoying the job she'd embarked
on so carelessly. That she would regret having
to resign in order to substantiate her harassment
claim.

In connection with this, she'd expected that by
now her involvement with him would have got
around via the usually efficient office grapevine,
adding weight to her eventual complaint against
him.

Every day, she went in prepared for knowing
looks, smothered grins, and whispered remarks.
But there was nothing. If anyone knew or even
suspected, they were keeping very quiet about it.

Maybe when he's going out with nobodies like Evie and myself, he prefers to keep his private life strictly under wraps, she thought, recalling that Evie hadn't featured in many of the pictures in the scrapbook. In fact, Tarn couldn't remember seeing even one, suggesting her foster sister had been told to stay off-camera when she appeared with him in public.

And she'd have been far too besotted to protest, or ask, 'Are you ashamed to be seen with me?' Tarn told herself bitterly.

She had phoned The Refuge several times, but the hoped-for permission to visit Evie was still being withheld, which worried her.

'That place really is like a prison,' she complained to Della, who shrugged.

'Maybe seclusion is what she most needs,' she returned. 'When my mother was in hospital last year, she said she'd have given every penny she possessed for a couple of days of peace, quiet and no visitors.' She added gently, 'I think, my pet, you have to give them credit for offering her the best possible treatment.'

'I suppose you're right,' Tarn conceded, sighing.

She wished very much that she hadn't left Evie's letters in New York. She'd have liked to check how long had elapsed between the first date with

Caz, and that delirious weekend alone with him in the depths of the country.

However, it couldn't be much longer before he made his move, she thought, biting her lip. No matter how circumspect and restrained his behaviour towards her, his eyes often told a different story, sending the unequivocal message that he wanted her.

It was moments like that which kept her awake at night, and made her question uneasily whether the shivers that ran through her at the thought of seeing him again were solely caused by apprehension.

If he has this effect on me without even trying, she mused wretchedly, how will I manage when he decides to get serious? If he ever does.

It was a question for which she had to find an answer sooner than she'd thought.

She was on her way down to the art department the following day, when she came face to face with him in an otherwise deserted corridor.

Caz stopped a few feet away from her, and she felt the hungry intensity of his gaze touch her like an electric charge. She stared back at him, aware of the sudden clamour of her pulses, knowing that if she took even a single step forward she would be in his arms.

But Caz stood his ground. Kept his distance. She saw his hands clench into fists at his side and swift colour flare along his cheekbones. He said abruptly, 'Dinner? Friday evening—at my flat?'

The moment of decision had arrived, catching her unprepared and suddenly hesitant.

You don't have to do this, said an urgent voice in her head. *You can take Della's advice, abandon the whole idea and run.*

For a moment, she had to struggle to think of Evie as she'd been on that first visit to The Refuge, but knew she needed to remember the small, broken figure in the bed, with the scared voice who was the reason why she'd embarked on this course of action, and why she had to go on to the inevitably bitter end.

Her mouth was dry. 'Yes,' she said. 'If—if that's what you want.'

'You must know that it is.' He paused, drawing a deep breath. 'I'll send Terry to pick you up at eight.'

She nodded. 'Eight o clock,' she said huskily. 'Yes.'

She moved to one side of the corridor, he to the other, and they continued on their respective ways without saying more.

Tarn however by-passed the art department,

heading instead for the women's cloakroom. She went straight to a basin, running the cold tap over her wrists, and wiping her face with a damp paper towel as she waited for her inner tumult to die down a little.

Two days and two nights, she thought, before she could achieve her aim and start the process which would make Caz Brandon the target of the contempt he deserved. He'd feature in some very different headlines before it was all finished.

She leaned against the basin, feeling faintly nauseated as she stared at her reflection in the mirror, face white, eyes glittering like a cat's.

She said under her breath, 'I look like a stranger. Worse than that—like someone I wouldn't want to know. I could even pose for a portrait—Nemesis, goddess of retribution.'

Only a few weeks ago, her life had been in place. Her career was fine, she was enjoying her sojourn in New York and she was in a relationship that might even have become love if she'd given it the chance.

Although at this moment, she found it hard to remember what Howard had looked like, let alone what it had meant to be held, kissed by him.

It seemed as if this thing with Evie had consumed her, leaving room for nothing else.

When it was over, she doubted whether she would return to the States for longer than it took to re-let her apartment and pack the rest of her things.

Maybe she'd take at least some of Della's advice and find a new home somewhere in Europe. France, maybe, or Italy. Or perhaps a Greek island. After all, the nature of her job meant she could work anywhere that she could set up her computer, so why didn't she take full advantage of the fact? Find her real self again in this new beginning.

But it was too soon to be making any decisions about the long-term when it was the immediate future which had to be foremost in her mind.

And right now, the art department was still waiting, so getting back to work was a priority. Time enough afterwards, when she got home, to consider all the implications of Caz's invitation, and how to deal with them.

She had the flat to herself on Friday evening, as Della was spending the weekend at her sister's house in Kent. She'd told her that she and Caz were having dinner but omitted further details, knowing exactly the objections that Della would raise. Knowing that nothing her friend could say would deflect her from her ultimate goal.

Tarn was glad too that she could be nervous without a witness, as she systematically tried on and discarded every dress in her wardrobe, eventually going back to her first choice, a simple wrap-round style in a jade-green silky fabric which clung unashamedly to her slender body.

She used cosmetics with a light hand, darkening her long lashes with mascara, and painting her mouth a soft, clear coral.

Nothing too overt, she told herself as she brushed her hair back from her face and secured it at the nape of her neck with an antique silver clasp.

Her legs were shaking under her as she walked down to the car. She sat huddled into a corner of the rear passenger seat, staring out at the busy London evening with eyes that saw nothing.

She wasn't even aware of the route Terry had taken, rousing herself only when the car drove through a security checkpoint and down a ramp to a private underground car park.

'The lift is here, madam. You press the button marked "P" for the penthouse, and "G" for the garage on your return. Mr Brandon will arrange for me to be waiting for you here by the lift gates.'

If his driver was staying on call, Caz could not be planning a lengthy seduction, she thought, her throat tightening. He must think he had her in the palm of his hand, she told herself, as she forced a smile and murmured her thanks.

She pressed the button and was swept smoothly and swiftly to the top floor of the building. As the lift doors slid open, she saw Caz descending a shallow flight of stairs at the other end of a carpeted corridor.

As he reached her, he said quietly, 'So you're here.'

'I thought you'd asked me.'

'I did. But with you I can never be certain.' He took her hand. 'Come and meet the others.'

Others? Tarn repeated silently, as she walked beside him. That was the last thing she'd expected to hear.

But, as they went up the stairs, she could hear music playing softly and the sound of voices.

She found herself in a vast lamplit room, and confronted by a huge picture window offering sweeping views of London by night.

On the right hand side of the room, two girls in neat black skirts and white blouses were putting the finishing touches to a circular table laid for four and gleaming with silver and crystal.

On the left hand side, three beautifully sculpted sofas upholstered in cream linen had been arranged round a fireplace, illumined by the glow of a gas fire.

All, she thought, exactly as Evie had described.

A tall fair man rose to his feet from one of the sofas, and waited smiling as Caz and Tarn approached. His companion was a dark, pretty girl, whose pale pink wool dress, although beautifully cut, did not completely conceal the fact that she was pregnant.

'Tarn, may I introduce the Donnells, two of my oldest friends. Brendan—Grace—this is Tarn Desmond.'

'It's good to meet you at last.' Brendan Donnell's handshake was firm, his blue eyes dancing. 'God knows, Caz has talked about little else.'

Tarn flushed. 'I'm sure that's an exaggeration.'

'Only a slight one,' said his wife. She patted the sofa. 'Come and sit beside me while Caz gets you a drink. I'm on the orange juice, sadly, although I'll allow myself a glass of wine at dinner, if Bren's not looking.'

Tarn was glad to sit, her mind still reeling from the scuppering of her plan for the evening. Before many minutes had passed, she'd learned that Brendan was managing director of the Lindsmore

Investment Group, that they had recently moved out of London to a house in the depths of rural Surrey, and that Grace, currently on maternity leave, had been a corporation lawyer.

'I planned to go back when the baby was born,' she confided. 'But now I'm not so sure. The house needs work and I'm really enjoying getting it all organised. And we have a garden too, with a small orchard, which has always been my dream. I see a total change of career looming.'

She paused. 'What about you, Tarn? Have you always worked on magazines?'

'For much of the time, yes,' Tarn returned evasively.

'And you and Caz met when you were job-hunting,' Grace said musingly. 'Now there's a lucky chance.'

At that moment, Caz returned with the white wine she'd asked for, so she was saved from having to reply and was able to smile rather tautly and thank him instead.

What the hell was he playing at—introducing her to his friends? she raged inwardly. And without a word of warning either so that she couldn't think of an excuse. It seemed out of place as well as out of character. She certainly couldn't remember Evie referring to anyone called Donnell in her letters, or noticed the name in her diary. And could these really be the powerful friends she'd been warned against? That also appeared unlikely. So what was happening? And what had he been saying about her?

But almost before she knew it, she was no longer having to pretend her enjoyment of making a new acquaintance, because it was impossible to harbour resentment over the collapse of her scheming when she was having such a good time.

Certainly the evening she'd planned had never included helpless laughter. Or eating very much for that matter.

Yet the dinner supplied by the very efficient catering company was wonderful too, from the excellent clear soup, through the flavoursome casserole of spring lamb with baby vegetables to the wickedly rich chocolate mousse and splendid cheese board. In spite of herself, Tarn found she was doing the meal full justice.

Also it was clear that Caz had never had any intention of attempting to move their relationship to a more intimate level, because Brendan and Grace were not vanishing when dinner was over, thus leaving them alone together, but apparently spending the night in his spare bedroom.

'I have some baby shopping to do in the morning,' Grace confided. 'So, it's a dual purpose visit.'

And so was mine, thought Tarn bleakly. Finding some way of luring him to disaster.

She let herself back into the empty flat, tossed her bag to one side and sank down on the sofa. The evening had not turned out at all as she expected, or planned for. In fact, a degree of re-thinking was called for.

Because now there were other even more disturbing factors to add to the mix…

The evening had ended pleasantly with coffee and brandy and more conversation on topics ranging from the serious to the frankly frivolous, and she'd experienced real reluctance when she looked at her watch and said that she must go.

'But we'll meet again.' Grace hugged her. 'I'll get Caz to bring you down to the hovel. Are you any kind of a photographer? You could take some before and after pictures—of me and the house,' she added with a giggle.

A nice thought, Tarn acknowledged silently. What a pity it could never happen.

Using her need to 'freshen up' as an excuse, she'd seen the rest of the flat, even managing a look at Caz's bedroom. The bed was indeed vast just as Evie had artlessly confided, and for a moment Tarn had been assailed by a disturbing image of the two of them naked and passionately entwined, Evie surrendering eagerly to every sensual demand that he made of her.

Tarn found herself backing away hastily, shutting her eyes, a little gasp that mingled pain with horror rasping her dry throat.

But thinking of them together was perhaps something she needed to do, she told herself, in order to counteract the unexpected pleasures of the evening, and remind her of the real reason why she'd accepted this invitation.

'So,' Caz said as he walked with her to the lift. 'Am I forgiven?'

She was momentarily startled. 'For what?'

'For changing tonight's rules of engagement.' He shook his head. 'There was a moment as you arrived when you looked as if you were about to face a firing squad.'

'Oh.' She took a breath. 'Well—hardly. Your friends are charming.'

'I'm glad you think so. They were also charmed.' He sent her a frowning glance. 'Yet suddenly here you are at a distance again. Why?'

Her heart missed a beat. 'You—you're imagining things.'

Caz said softly, 'Prove it,' and took her in his arms.

For an instant, his face seemed to swim before her startled eyes, then his mouth came down on hers, and not in the customary fleeting graze of a kiss that she expected either. She'd learned to deal with that, after a fashion. But this time his intentions were clearly very different. He was there to stay.

Her first instinct was to brace her hands against his chest and push him away, because her own intentions were entirely different too. Yet what logical reason did she have to remain aloof? Reason indicated that by now she should at least appear to want to be in his arms, and that any form of resistance might simply lead to him giving up the chase, which would destroy her ultimate objective. Having come so far, could she really risk that?

Besides, in practical terms, the way he was holding her suggested that fighting him would be like trying to push over a brick wall.

Because his lips might still be gentle as they explored hers, but they were also warm and unashamedly determined, and they demanded a response. The desire she'd seen in his eyes had now become a physical reality.

Prove it...

Warning her quite explicitly that he was tired of waiting. That the next step was there to be taken.

In the full and certain consciousness of this, she let her mouth move under his slowly and sweetly, offering him a reply that was shy but willing.

His fingers were tangling in her hair, unfastening the silver clip and letting the scented strands tumble over her shoulders.

He sighed against her mouth and his kiss deepened, his tongue probing her lips, seeking her surrender to a new and disturbing intimacy.

Tarn was not aware of moving, but suddenly her body seemed to sink into his, one hand on his shoulder, the other cupping the nape of his neck as her lips parted for him.

Then, between one heartbeat and the next, she was lost, the scent of him, the taste of him swamping her astonished senses, as her tongue lapped almost frantically against his, and her teeth grazed his mouth in turn.

They swayed together, his hands sliding down to her hips, pulling her even closer. She could feel the hardness of him against her thighs, triggering a sweet drenching surge of longing in her own body, which sent shock waves to her reeling mind by its very intensity.

Caz raised his head, looking down at her, his

eyes burning under half-closed lids as he studied her flushed face.

His hand swept the dress from her shoulder, and he bent to kiss her bared skin, his lips tracing the delicacy of her bone structure, before moving down to the lace which shrouded her breast, and closing on the deep rose of her nipple, suckling it with sensuous delight.

Tarn's head fell back and she moaned softly at this unfamiliar mingling of pain and pleasure. Every sense, every nerve-ending she possessed was in turmoil, warning her that if he was to push her back against the wall and take her, she would not be able to deny him.

And suddenly she was more afraid than she'd ever been in her life. More even than of being sent away from Wilmont Road as an unwanted child again. Because she had never felt like this before. Never experienced the blazing force of sheer physical need. The overwhelming urge to be taken and give endlessly in return.

But that would ruin everything. She couldn't jettison her aims for the brief satisfaction of the moment. She had to retrieve the lost ground and resist him. Had to…

'Caz—no.' Her voice was small and husky. 'Stop—please. You—I can't…'

For a breathless moment, she thought her protest was going to be ignored, then, slowly and reluctantly, he straightened.

Taking a deep, steadying breath, he restored her dress to order, then ran a finger down the heated curve of her cheek in a gesture that was as much reassuring as tender.

He said very quietly, 'Are you telling me you don't want me?'

Mutely, she shook her head, knowing it would be useless to attempt to lie.

'Then what is it? Has someone in the past treated you badly—hurt you?'

How can you ask that? she wanted to cry aloud. You of all people? Where was all the gentleness and concern for Evie?

'Tell me, sweetheart, was it this guy in the States?'

'Howard?' It was a struggle now even to remember his name, she thought with shame. 'No, it's nothing like that. Quite the opposite, in fact.' She swallowed. 'It's just that I don't... I haven't— ever...' She stumbled to a halt, staring down at the carpet. 'Ludicrous, isn't it?'

Caz said gravely, 'Do you hear me laughing?' He shook his head. 'My darling, being a virgin isn't some kind of stigma. And, anyway, I should have realised. It explains some of the contradictions I've sensed in you.'

He took her back into his arms, holding her close, his cheek resting on her hair. 'So, at some future time might I be able to persuade you to reconsider your present stance?'

'I don't know.' And that, too, was no more than the truth. 'I—I'm so confused.'

'Then it looks as if I'll just have to go on waiting,' he said. 'And hoping…'

Remembering his words, the wry husky tone of his voice, sent a slow voluptuous whisper of sensation rippling through her body. She found herself remembering his hands—his mouth. Felt her flesh stir—her breathing quicken…

'Oh, God,' she whispered. 'Of all the men in the world, Caz Brandon, why must you be the one to make me feel like this? When you're the one who needs to be driven crazy with unfulfilled desire.'

And knew that in order to defeat him, she faced the fight of her life.

CHAPTER SEVEN

'It's not fair,' Mrs Griffiths complained fretfully. 'All this talk about human rights, and I can't even see my own daughter.' She gave Tarn a mulish stare. 'It's about time you did something.'

'I have tried.' Tarn made herself speak gently. She'd spent a restless night interspersed with wild and disturbing dreams, then woken very early when the sky was barely streaked with light to discover with shock that her arms were wrapped round her pillow, holding it closely to her body as if it were flesh and blood rather than feathers and down. And realised that she was glad she couldn't remember her dreams in detail.

She'd known from past experience that she would not go back to sleep, yet was unwilling to simply lie there, staring into space, while she reviewed yet again the events of the previous evening and tried to make sense of them. Or rationalise her reaction to them.

Instead, she'd got up, dragged on some track suit

bottoms and a T-shirt, and conducted a cleaning blitz on the flat, losing herself in sheer physical hard work.

When she'd finished, the whole place gleamed and she surveyed it with a sense of real satisfaction.

She showered and washed her hair, then, with the faintest hint of gritted teeth, she reminded herself that she almost certainly owed her foster mother a visit and took a bus to Wilmont Road before heading off to the supermarket for the Saturday morning shop.

'But clearly you haven't tried hard enough.' Mrs Griffiths was like a dog with a bone, and not to be put off. 'I need her, and Evie needs me at a time like this. You have to tell those doctors so. You must.'

I can talk to the Professor until I'm blue in the face, but it won't make the slightest difference, Tarn thought, suppressing a sigh. Aloud, she said temperately, 'I'll go down there tomorrow and see what I can do.'

'I've bought her a dress,' Mrs Griffiths said. 'Her favourite turquoise. And I want to give it to her myself. Tell them that. Make it perfectly clear.'

Tarn nodded as she got up from the kitchen table and walked to the door, where she paused as a thought struck her. 'Talking of clothes, what happened to Evie's wedding dress? Is it here somewhere, because there was no sign of it at the flat. I don't want her to ask me about it, and not be able to answer her.'

Aunt Hazel shook her head. 'I don't know, I'm sure. I certainly never saw it. Another of her surprises, poor baby. But when she described it, I wasn't convinced that satin was the wisest choice she could have made.'

'I think that was probably the least of her worries,' Tarn said, then stopped, her brows drawing together in a swift frown. 'Did you say it was satin? I thought—she said in one of her letters that it was cream lace and chiffon.'

'Satin,' said Aunt Hazel. 'And oyster. I think she looked at quite a few before she made up her mind.'

'Yes,' Tarn acknowledged, still frowning. 'I suppose that must be it.'

'And you'll go down to see her. You won't let that Della talk you into doing something else.'

'Della's away this weekend, visiting her family,' Tarn said with faint weariness.

Mrs Griffiths sniffed. 'Well, aren't they the lucky ones. Of course, I should have insisted you stay here instead of moving in with that flighty piece.' She paused, giving Tarn a critical stare. 'As it is, you look as if you've been burning the candle at both ends for a week.'

Tarn bit her lip. 'I simply had a bad night, that's all.'

'Just the same, I expect you slept better than my poor girl, locked away like that,' was Mrs Griffiths' parting shot, accompanying Tarn down the hall to the front door.

What happened to Evie was not my fault, she wanted to shout back. *But I'm doing my damnedest to make amends anyway.*

Instead, she bit her tongue hard and went shopping.

An hour and two heavy bags later, she let herself into the apartment block and walked up the single flight of stairs to the flat. As she reached the landing, a tall figure moved away from the wall he'd been leaning against and came towards her.

'I was just about to leave you a note,' said Caz.

Tarn, aware that her jaw had dropped, hurriedly restored it to its proper level, thankful he could not hear the tattoo that her pulse was drumming.

As she'd pushed her trolley up and down the aisles, she'd been rehearsing what she would say, how she would behave when she next saw him. Now here he was, lithe and attractive in pale chinos and a dark blue shirt, its sleeves rolled back over his tanned forearms, its open neck revealing a dark shadowing of chest hair.

And suddenly her wits seemed to have deserted her.

She said with an assumption of cool, 'And what was the note going to say?'

'It's a lovely day. Let's spend it together.'

'Brief and to the point.' She swallowed past the dryness in her throat. The nervous twist in her stomach. 'But what about your friends?'

'They're going to have a short, sharp shop, then get back to Surrey. Grace tires easily these days.'

'Yes, I suppose she would.' Tarn forced a smile. 'The perils of motherhood.'

His tone was laconic. 'It's reckoned to have its compensations too.' He paused. 'So will you come with me?' He added softly, 'We can treat it as a journey of discovery.'

Tarn hesitated. 'I'll have to put my shopping away.'

'Of course.'

'And change.' She glanced down at her black cut-offs and crisp white blouse, thankful that the track suit and tee of her cleaning marathon had been safely consigned to the laundry basket.

'Unnecessary,' he said. 'What more do you

need for a trip to the seaside? Apart from a jacket, maybe.'

This time her smile was genuine if a little startled. 'The coast? That would be lovely.'

'You unpack your groceries,' he said. 'I'll make coffee and we'll argue about whether to go south or east. The Channel or the North Sea.'

She nodded. 'Fine,' and unlocked the door.

'You've been busy,' Caz commented as he followed her into the spotless kitchen.

'I enjoy housework.' Which was just as well, she reflected, as she'd certainly done enough of it when she was living at Wilmont Road. She began to empty the first bag. 'If all else fails I can always apply to the MacNaughton Company for a job.'

'I used them at one time.' Caz filled the kettle, set it to boil and found the cafetière. 'But I'm not sure I'd recommend them. Anyway, who's talking about failure?'

She passed him the fresh pack of coffee she'd just bought, telling herself that Evie must have obtained the paperwork about the cleaning company from him. Something she should have realised. Aloud, she said, 'No-one can predict the future.'

'I can.' He took the coffee from her, and held onto her hand, looking down at the palm and tracing a line with his fingertip. 'And I foresee a long and happy life.'

His touch shivered through her senses as if his hand had stroked her naked body.

She detached herself with a self-conscious laugh. 'I don't believe in fortune telling.'

'Not even when the fortune is being arranged for you?'

'Particularly not then.' She made her tone crisp. Continued putting things away in cupboards. Did not look at him.

'In other words, I'm rushing you into something you're not ready for. *Mea culpa.*' He paused. 'Is that why you looked again as if you were confronting your worst nightmare when you saw me just now?'

'I was just surprised, that's all.' In order to reach the fridge, she would have to get past him, so she put the items for cold storage on one side. 'I—I wasn't expecting to see you so soon.'

The dark brows lifted sardonically. 'Really?' He spooned coffee into the cafetière. 'I thought I'd made my intentions pretty clear.'

Tarn shrugged. 'Perhaps I'm having trouble believing that you have any intentions.'

He gave her a swift grin. 'For someone who

doesn't like to be rushed, lady, that sounds sus-
piciously like a hint for a declaration.'

'No—nothing like that.' Her protest was instant.
'It's just that— Oh, for heaven's sake, everyone
knows that you're involved with Ginny Fraser.
And how many others before her? How many so-
called declarations have there been?'

*Tell me about Evie. Offer some explanation—
express some compunction for what you've done
to her. I'm giving you this chance...*

He said quietly, 'I've never pretended I've lived
like a Trappist monk while waiting for the right
woman to walk into my life. Ginny had her career
and I had mine. Our relationship has been—convenient. It is now in the past.'

Consigned to oblivion—like Evie.

She watched him fill the cafetière with boiling
water, her hands curling into fists at her sides. She
said, 'But Ginny wasn't the only one. What about
the others? What happened to them?'

'You're beginning to make me feel like Bluebeard,'
he commented unsmilingly. 'All I can tell you is
that I never made any woman a promise I wasn't
prepared to keep. And that, my lovely one, will
also apply to you.' He paused. 'Now shall we relax
a little and discuss how to spend our day?'

* * *

In the end, they drove to Whytecliffe, a village on the South coast set on a small bay.

She'd been surprised to find a sleek black convertible two-seater parked a few yards from the apartment block.

'No Terry?' she asked.

'A driver is more convenient on working days. But at weekends, I like to drive myself. And as I said—we're spending the day together.' He slanted a smile at her. 'Don't you trust me to take care of you?'

'Of course.' But, in truth, she wasn't altogether sure. This car looked to have a lot of power under its pared-down lines.

Hood down, they headed out of the city, and Tarn soon realised she hadn't the least cause for concern. He was a terrific driver, positive without being aggressive, treating other road-users with consideration.

'So where are we going?' she asked as they left the suburbs behind.

'It's a surprise.'

And a very pleasant one, she discovered, as they eventually wound their way through narrow lanes with the sea shining in front of them, and reached Whytecliffe.

It was small and sleepy in comparison to other

nearby resorts, its harbour catering primarily for private sailing dinghies rather than the fishing smacks of the past, while further round the bay, at the foot of the chalk cliff, a row of brightly painted beach huts stood sentinel over the stretch of sand and pebbles leading down to the sea.

The village itself had a Norman church, and a pleasant main street, partly cobbled, which housed a few shops and cafés. They walked slowly, her hand in his because he'd reached for it and she couldn't think of a solitary reason to deny him, looking into the windows of the various antique shops, as they went and wandering round the small gallery displaying the work of local artists.

There was also a bistro-type restaurant which turned out to be only open in the evenings, but Caz declared that was unimportant and headed for the solitary pub overlooking the breakwater.

'The Smuggler's Chair.' Tarn looked up at the swinging sign above the door. 'That's a strange name.'

'And it goes with a strange story.' Caz had to bend to negotiate the low entrance. He guided Tarn down a tiled passage and through a door with 'Fisherman's Catch' painted on it.

She found herself in a wood panelled room, with

old-fashioned settles flanking tables set for lunch, several of which were already occupied.

Caz ordered a white wine spritzer for her and a beer for himself, and they took the remaining table by the window.

The menu was chalked on a board, offering Dover sole, hake, crab and lobster, but they agreed to share the special, a seafood platter served with a mixed green salad and crusty bread.

'So tell me about the Smuggler's Chair,' Tarn said when their order had been given.

'Well, in the bad old days, the village had a reputation for being involved in free-trading,' Caz said. 'And cargoes from France were regularly landed here.

'The leader of the gang used to come here to drink quite openly—apparently he had an eye for the landlord's daughter—and he always sat in the same chair by the fire.

'An informer told the Excisemen who organised a surprise raid. When they burst in, there was this man sitting in the chair with his pipe and his pint pot, just as they'd been told. They ordered him to stay still, but he reached into his coat, and thinking he was going for his pistol, they shot him.

'However, when they searched the body, they found government papers authorising him to compile a secret report on the local free trade. It seems the smugglers had their own informers, and were expecting his visit.

'Which is why, when he arrived at the inn, he was made welcome—and offered the best chair by the parlour fire.'

'Nasty.' Tarn wrinkled her nose. 'What happened to the gang leader?'

Caz shrugged. 'Got away, scot-free, and presumably found somewhere else to drink, complete with some other obliging wench.'

'And the chair?'

'Oh, that's allegedly still here in the other bar, but it seems no-one fancied using it after the shooting in case the Excisemen returned and made a second mistake, so it was always left empty, and the story got around that it was haunted, and that doom and disaster would pursue anyone reckless enough to sit there. Even these days, it's given a wide berth.'

Tarn laughed. 'You surely don't believe that.'

'I heard the story at a very impressionable age,' Caz said solemnly. 'My parents used to rent a house nearby for the holidays. The then landlord used to offer a fiver to anyone who'd take the risk. I gather it's currently gone up to a hundred quid, but still no takers.'

Tarn took a reflective sip of her spritzer. 'It's quite a reward—just for sitting down. I think I might try it.'

Caz put down his glass. 'No.' The negative was sharp and held a note of finality.

'Oh, for heaven's sake,' she said laughing. 'It probably isn't even the same chair.'

'Possibly not,' Caz agreed. 'That doesn't change a thing.'

Tarn gave a provocative whistle. 'Palmistry, now superstition,' she marvelled teasingly. 'I would never have believed it. But you were quite right,' she added. 'This is certainly a voyage of discovery.'

'Nothing of the kind,' he returned. 'If you sit in the smuggler's chair and lightning fails to strike, you've ruined a perfectly good legend forever, and it'll be the landlord's curse you need to watch out for if you spoil his trade.'

'The pragmatic response,' Tarn said lightly. 'I'm disappointed. But I suppose you're right.'

'Besides,' Caz went on thoughtfully. 'Disasters I can well do without.'

'Ah,' she said. 'But I'd be the one to suffer.'

'Not any more,' he said. 'What happens to you, happens to me. That's the way it is, lady.'

Tarn looked down at the table, her heart hammering. *Dear God,* she said silently, *please don't let that work both ways. Not this time.*

The seafood platter was piled high with prawns, mussels, oysters, cockles, spider crabs and crayfish, and came with finger bowls and a pile of paper napkins.

Sharing it with him should have been a problem, an intimacy she could have done without, but in some strange way it was fine, even enjoyable, as if they'd been doing it all their lives.

And, at the same time, it was messy, funny and totally delicious.

Of all the meals we've eaten together, she thought suddenly, this is the one I shall always remember. And stopped right there, because she didn't want any memories of him to take, alone again, into the next chapter of her life. Because she couldn't afford that kind of weakness.

They decided to forego the desserts, choosing instead a pot of good, strong coffee.

'Shall we take a walk along the beach before the tide turns?' Caz suggested, as he paid the bill.

There was flat sand beyond the pebbles and shingle, and the sea was just a murmur, its surface barely ruffled by the breeze. Tarn drew the clean air deep into her lungs as she lifted her face to the sun, wondering at the same time how things would be if nothing existed but this moment.

'So, tell me what you did in New York.' He spoke softly, but his question brought her sharply back to reality. Because it was clear he expected to be answered.

She shrugged. 'I suppose—pretty much what I do now.'

'Your editor was sorry to lose you.'

'I owe her a lot.' *Especially for that reference.*

'Will the job be waiting for you—if you go back?'

'That or another one. I've rarely been out of work.' She didn't want the interrogation to continue, so she bent, slipping off her loafers. 'I'm going to find out if the sea is as inviting as it looks,' she threw over her shoulder as she headed for the crescent of ripples unfolding on the sand.

'I warn you now—it will be cold,' Caz called after her, amused.

'You can't scare me. I've been to Cape Cod,' she retorted, speeding into a run.

He hadn't been joking, she discovered. The chill made her catch her breath and stand gasping for a moment, but an ignominious retreat back to the beach was out of the question for all kinds of reasons. So she waded in a little deeper, finding that it grew more bearable with every step, until eventually it bordered on pleasure.

However, it was also bordering on the turn-ups of her linen pants, which was not part of the plan at all, so she opted for discretion over valour and walked slowly back to the shore.

Caz looked at her, shaking his head in mock outrage. 'Crazy woman.'

She lifted her chin. 'Chicken!'

'But not a chicken risking pneumonia. Or with wet feet and no towel.' Before she could stop him, he picked her up in his arms and carried her up the beach, scrunching over the pebbles before setting her down on a large, flat rock. 'I prefer my seas warm, like the Mediterranean or around the Maldives.'

He produced a spotless white handkerchief from a pocket in his chinos and unfolded it. 'I'm afraid this is the best we can do.' He dropped to one knee in front of Tarn and began to dry her feet, slowly, gently and with immense care. 'Like blocks of stone, as my old nanny would have said. Even your nail polish has turned blue.'

Forbidding herself to laugh, she tried to free herself. 'There's no need for this. I can manage—really.'

'Is it the reference to Nanny that's worrying

you?' Caz looked up at her, his hazel eyes warm and amused. 'Do you think I'm going to revert to childhood and play "This little piggy"? Or are you afraid I'm a secret foot fetishist seizing his opportunity?'

'It's just—inappropriate,' Tarn managed lamely, aware that some totally foreign instinct was prompting her to wriggle her toes into the palm of his hand, and not just for warmth either.

'Is it?' He was grinning openly now. 'I do hope so. I'd hate to be politically correct at a moment like this.' He traced the delicate bone structure of her slender toes with the tip of a finger. Cupped the softness of her heel. 'They're adorable,' he said softly. 'Maybe these foot fetishists have a point.'

'Caz.' Her voice was husky. 'Don't—please.'

'Why not? Isn't this where women like to see men—kneeling at their feet?'

'I am not "women".' Tarn could feel that betraying heat spreading through her body again. 'And I want to put my shoes on.'

'In a minute. This is a new experience for me, and I like it.' He bent his head and kissed each instep, warmly and lingeringly. 'They taste of salt,' he whispered.

The breath caught in her throat. She said with

difficulty, 'People—there are people coming. You must get up.'

Caz shook his head. 'And lose this perfect opportunity? Not a chance.' He looked up at her, and there was no laughter in his gaze. It was serious and intent. 'Tarn, my sweet, my lovely girl, will you marry me?'

'You—you said you wouldn't rush me.' Her voice was a whisper too.

'I dare not wait,' he said quietly. 'After all, you came out of nowhere. I'm terrified that you may disappear in the same way.'

'No,' she said. 'I—I won't do that. But it's too soon. You must see that.' She spread her hands almost beseechingly. 'We—we hardly know each other.'

'Something I'm seriously trying to redress,' he said. 'Or hadn't you noticed? Sweetheart, we can catch up on the details as we go. But I think I knew from that first moment that you were the one. I guess it was too much to hope that you felt the same.'

He added almost harshly, 'But now that I've found you, Tarn, I can't let you go, and I won't. Not when I love you and want you to be my wife. You and no-one else for the rest of our lives.'

'This isn't fair...'

'I think there's a cliché that covers that—something about love and war.'

But this is war, she cried out silently, from the pain and confusion inside her. *It's just that you don't know it yet.*

Aloud, she said, stumbling over her words, 'I—I have to think. You must give me time. We have to be sure.'

Caz sighed ruefully. 'My darling, I am sure. Now, I just have to convince you. But I'll be patient. I won't even ask if you love me in return. Or not yet.'

He took her loafers and fitted them back on to her feet. 'There you go, Cinderella. They fit. Now you can't turn me down.'

'You may believe you're Prince Charming,' Tarn said, forcing herself somehow to speak lightly as she scrambled up from her rock. Struggling to behave as if the whole world had not turned upside down. 'But this couple walking their dog probably think you're an escaped lunatic.'

Caz turned towards the elderly man and woman, walking arm in arm along the beach, their Jack Russell scampering ahead of them. 'Good afternoon,' he called. 'Isn't this a wonderful day?'

The man looked dubiously at the sky. 'I reckon we've had the best of it, and it's clouding over for rain. The weather's always treacherous at this time of year.'

Treacherous, thought Tarn. Why had this man, this stranger, chosen that of all words?

'Darling, you're shivering, and our coats are in the car.' Caz spoke with compunction. He untied the sweater looped casually around his shoulders. 'Wear this.'

Obediently, Tarn pulled the enveloping softness over her head, knowing as she did so that the freshening breeze from the sea was not the problem, and that a dozen layers of cashmere would never be enough to alleviate the icy numbness building inside her. Possessing her. Making her feel she would never be warm again.

Oh, God, she thought desperately. What have I done? And what am I doing? I don't seem to know any more.

Worst of all, I'm not sure I know myself. And that terrifies me.

CHAPTER EIGHT

It was a largely silent journey back to London.

Caz was quietly attentive, asking if she was warm enough, or if she'd like to listen to some music. Tarn assented politely to both propositions, hoping that the second option would avoid any more discussion of his plans for their future. However, she declined a further suggestion that they should stop somewhere for tea.

She wanted to get back, she thought, because she needed to think. To work out what to do next. If that was possible.

The CD he picked featured a woman singer she did not recognise, with a deep, almost harsh bluesy voice, whose lyrics were, without exception, a disturbing exploration of love, and all its confusing complexities.

Something else Tarn could well have done without.

She told herself that everything Caz had said to her on the beach was entirely meaningless and just part of a well-worn routine. That he'd probably gone on his knees to Evie in exactly the same way.

Yet, in spite of all that, she could still remember how the look in his eyes had made her breathless and the way his smile had reached out to touch her. Could feel the clasp of his hand round hers as they returned to the car, strong and sure as if he would never let her go, and catch the familiar scent of his cologne on the sweater she was still wearing.

Which, of course, she could return. Disposing of all those other sensations was an entirely different matter.

How, she asked silently, was it possible for him to sound so sincere? To almost make her believe…

She stopped right there. That was not a line she needed to follow.

Although for him to want her had been, of course, an essential part of her plan. She'd intended to rouse him to a fever pitch of unsatisfied desire, before slamming him into limbo, harshly and very publicly. And thanks to Lisa, she'd already worked out the perfect occasion.

'Each June, there's a garden party at a house called Winsleigh Place,' her editor had told her. 'Everyone in the company is invited from the directors to the cleaners and catering staff. Coaches are laid on to take us all there and back, so no-one is tempted to drink and drive. There's a wonderful buffet lunch, with non-stop champagne, and in the evening, a dance, with more glorious food. And Caz provides it all.'

So the entire Brandon ensemble would hear the unpleasant truth about their supposed Lord Bountiful, Tarn had resolved, even as she smiled and said with perfect truth, 'It sounds perfect.'

But today's turn of events had thrown her scheme back into the melting pot. If she refused his proposal, she would have revenge of a sort, but it would be a private matter between the two of them, and she wanted more than that.

On the other hand, if she agreed, then she would almost certainly attend the garden party as his fiancée, and any attempt to discredit him would reflect just as badly on her. People would wonder how she could possibly have become engaged to him, knowing what she did.

And I wouldn't be able to answer them, she thought.

Unless, of course, he intended to keep her under wraps until he was tired of her, as he'd clearly done with Evie. A thought that twisted inside her like a knife.

But even that possibility seemed totally unable

to negate any of the feelings towards him that had taken such an astonishing and unwelcome hold on her almost from the beginning, and intensified so alarmingly over the last forty-eight hours.

She felt as if two entirely different women were occupying her skin and fighting for the domination of her mind. And she had to make sure that the right one became the ultimate winner.

Because she could not let herself be beguiled by the sensuous passion of his mouth, or give way to the kind of impulse which had almost led her to stroke the dark silk of his hair as he knelt at her feet.

Nor could she allow herself to forget that, in the end, she'd been saved, not by her own strength of will, but by an amateur weather forecaster with a Jack Russell terrier.

And how shameful was that? she thought bitterly.

Della had once asked how she might have reacted to Caz if they'd simply met as strangers without Evie's involvement, and she'd replied dismissively, defensively.

If she asked me the same question now, she thought, I don't know what I'd say.

When they eventually reached her flat, Caz left the engine running as he turned and gave her a long, steady look. 'I'm not going to ask if I can come up with you,' he said quietly. 'Because I know damned well that I'd try a different kind of persuasion—in bed. And that wouldn't be right or fair.'

She bit her lip. 'Thank you. I want you to know that, whatever happens, you've given me the loveliest day.' She reached for the door handle, and hesitated. 'Oh—your sweater...'

'Keep it,' he said. His smile was faintly crooked. 'It looks far better on you than it ever did on me.' He paused. 'When you've made up your mind, whichever way it goes, call me.'

'Yes.'

'And I don't trust myself to kiss you either, in case you're wondering.'

Her own attempt to smile was a failure. 'You're—very strong-minded.'

'No,' he said. 'It's just that I feel I've put quite enough pressure on you already.' He ran a finger down the curve of her cheek. Touched it briefly to her mouth. 'Promise me we'll talk soon?'

She nodded, dry-mouthed, and left the car.

She didn't watch him drive away. She walked upstairs, aware that her legs were shaking. Fumbled the key into the lock. Closed the door behind her and leaned against it, staring blind-eyed into space, aware of little but the deep, rapid thud of her heart.

She was thankful that she was alone. That she could keep the day's events to herself, without having to offer excuses or explanations, because she could imagine what Della's reaction would be to this latest development.

Eventually, she forced herself to move. To walk to the kitchen and put on a pot of strong coffee to brew, while she took a shower. All sensible measures to dispel the ice which had apparently settled inside her.

But while the shower warmed her, it failed to make her feel any cleaner, so its comfort was, at best, limited, she thought wearily as she dried herself.

Wrapped in her dressing gown, she curled into a corner of the sofa, sipped her scalding coffee and tried to force her teeming brain to focus. She caught sight of her bare feet, and, realising that she was shivering voluptuously at the memories they evoked, hastily tucked them away under the skirts of her robe.

How was it possible, she wondered dazedly, for all that apparent tenderness, all that caring to be only an illusion?

She wished she still had the diary, which might

give her some clue as to what to expect next. After all, didn't they say that forewarned was fore-armed?

Unless his proposal was simply a ploy to get her into bed. A form of deception Caz hadn't needed with poor Evie, she thought bitterly. But if he thought she was merely playing hard to get, he would soon discover his mistake.

But just suppose that he means it, said a small sly voice in her brain. That, no matter what has happened in the past, you're the one that he truly wants. How do you deal with that?

I tell myself that it doesn't change a thing, she whispered under her breath. *And I keep saying it.*

Because if he was genuine, why didn't he tell me about Evie? Express some remorse for the way he treated her. Why didn't he say, 'Darling, I have something to confess. I was engaged once before to a sweet girl, but it didn't work out, and, although it's over, I know I hurt her terribly, and I shall always regret that.'

But he'd said nothing. Instead he's simply air-brushed her out of his life, she thought. And he could do the same to me. I must not ever let myself forget that.

She tried to divert herself by watching television. One of her favourite films was showing, something so familiar that she could almost repeat the dialogue by heart, but this evening it totally failed to engage her.

The scene on the beach unfolded, frame by frame, over and over again in her mind, eclipsing anything on the screen.

'Oh, to hell with it,' she muttered eventually. 'I'm going to bed.'

Her clothes were still lying on the bedroom floor, and she bent to retrieve them, tossing each item into the basket for laundering. Wondering, as she did so, whether she could ever bear to wear any of them again.

Until, at the bottom of the pile, she came upon Caz's sweater.

For a moment, she stared down at it, then, obeying some incomprehensible primal instinct, she gathered up its soft weight with both hands and held it against her breasts, her throat, her mouth, breathing in the scent of his skin, and drawing it deep into her lungs as if, by this means, she could somehow capture the essence of him and hold it within her forever.

A long, quivering sigh convulsed her body. A sigh of yearning, bewildering her with its strength. A sigh of loss and regret, and she felt her throat muscles tighten painfully as she tasted the first bitterness of tears. A low, animal sound rose from deep inside her and was torn from her parted lips.

And with it came chaos.

She sank down on to the carpet, still clutching the bundle of cashmere and pressing it to her face as if she hoped it could somehow staunch the tears that were pouring down her face, or silence the harsh, gasping sobs that were suddenly ripping her apart.

She seemed incapable of movement or even coherent thought as she crouched there, her body shaking uncontrollably.

I want him. I love him. Oh, God forgive me, I love him so much…

The words, unbelievable, unutterable, ran crazily through her head, piercing her with their shame.

When at long last there were no tears left, and her throat was aching with dry sobs, she got clumsily to her feet. She shed her robe and climbed naked into bed, spreading the damp sweater across her pillow and pressing her cheek against it. Knowing that it might be all she would ever have of him.

'From that first moment…'

His words, and she could see now that they were as true for her as he'd claimed they were for him.

That she'd gone to the reception looking only to avenge Evie and come away with her mind in turmoil, no matter how much she might have tried to deny it.

She could recognise now that she'd been in one form of denial or another ever since.

Something which had to stop right here. Because there were choices to be made, and she would need a clear head to make them, she thought as she closed her eyes and allowed herself to sink down into the mattress. Aware that very soon her physical and emotional exhaustion would take her over the edge into temporary oblivion, and let sleep work its magic.

She woke the next morning feeling calm and strangely empty, but knowing exactly what she had to do.

She would visit Evie at The Refuge that afternoon, no matter what obstacles were put in her way, and break the news to her that she had changed her mind and abandoned the planned revenge. At the same time, she would also tell her that she was leaving Britain, probably for good, and returning to her own life.

Because Della had been completely right, of course, she told herself. She had no obligation to drop everything and run to their aid whenever Aunt Hazel or Evie sent out an SOS. As it was, her intervention, however well-meant, had led to her own heartbreak, and she would need time and distance for the healing process to begin.

Evie, too, was receiving the best treatment and would also recover. And both she and her mother would eventually learn to stand on their own feet too.

I've done them no favours by encouraging their dependency, she thought.

Ironically, it was Caz himself who had shown her the only solution to this maze of lies and un-happiness she was embroiled in. After all, he'd said yesterday that she'd come out of nowhere and might vanish in the same way.

And that was precisely her intention. To depart without trace. To find somewhere else to live and sink back into her work. To start over, a chame-leon, invisible in her surroundings.

A clean break, she resolved, removing the ne-cessity for any tortuous and impossible expla-nations which would not reflect credit on either Caz or herself. 'Least said, soonest mended,' she thought wryly, and all the other comforting cli-chés, which were no comfort at all.

And if, at the moment, the break felt more like an amputation, she knew that once the numbness had worn off, the pain would start in earnest.

But maybe she could arrange to be long gone by then.

And in the meantime, ordinary life pursued its prosaic path.

She showered, dressed, and breakfasted on toast and coffee before making a bacon and sweetcorn quiche for Della's return at suppertime, just as she'd intended to do before her life skidded sideways to disaster.

She had also determined to return Evie's engagement ring anonymously to Caz. A padded envelope with a London postmark would give no clues. It was a reminder of unhappiness that the younger girl didn't need, she thought as she looked down at the cold glitter of the stones, as well as an awful warning of how easy it was to be dazzled into believing the improbable.

A danger that she herself was avoiding by a whisker.

While Caz—he can hand it on to the next lady who takes his fancy, she thought sinking her teeth into her lower lip, as she closed the box.

* * *

Professor Wainwright regarded Tarn with open disfavour. 'I thought we had an agreement, young lady. No visits without a prior appointment.'

'Yes,' she said. 'But I really do need to see her.'

'You are not the only one. Her visiting time today is already reserved.'

'I could wait…'

'Miss Griffiths may well find the experience—unsettling, and will need to rest.' He looked at his computer screen. 'Perhaps next week.'

'That's too late. I may not be here.' She paused. 'Please, Professor. I must at least be allowed to say goodbye to Evie.'

'But not today.' His tone was final. He began to put papers into a file. 'Now you must excuse me. I have a meeting.'

'Is there really no other time for me to see her?'

He sighed, and looked back at the screen. 'Tomorrow afternoon might be a possibility.'

'Yes,' she said. 'I'll come tomorrow.'

'But telephone first,' he cautioned. 'Her condition will need to be carefully assessed.'

'Very well,' Tarn said tonelessly, and rose.

'Miss Griffiths.' She was halfway to the door when his voice halted her. 'Since our last meeting have you told anyone of Evelyn's whereabouts?

Mentioned it inadvertently in conversation, perhaps?'

Tarn frowned. 'No, of course not.'

'Then there must be some other explanation.' He gave a brisk nod. 'I regret you've had another wasted journey.'

'Not really wasted,' she returned. 'Because I shall see Evie tomorrow.'

She could have walked back to the Parkway, but when she got to the main door, an elderly couple were paying off the station taxi, so she decided to ride there instead.

She had just settled herself into a corner of the back seat when another car came up the drive and stopped in a swirl of gravel.

More visitors, thought Tarn. And aren't they the lucky ones?

Then she saw the driver emerge and walk round to the rear passenger door, and stiffened incredulously.

Because she knew him. And the car. Knew, as well, with sick foreboding, exactly who his passenger must be.

She shrank back in her seat, every nerve-ending jangling, and pressed a clenched fist against her lips, stifling any hint of shocked and aching sound, as Caz got out and stood for a moment in the sunlight, clearly giving Terry instructions.

He was back to formality today, in a dark suit, and even carrying a brief case.

Legal documents? Papers for Evie to sign, enjoining her silence? Drawing a line under the past so he could look to the future with a free mind?

How can he? she whispered silently. *Oh, God, how can he do this to her? Force himself back into her life when she's trying to recover from the way he treated her. When what she needs more than anything is to wipe him from her memory forever.*

And I—how could I possibly have forgotten what he was and let myself be tempted by him, even for a moment?

She felt physically ill as she watched him walk up the steps and disappear inside the building. She hadn't been allowed in, Aunt Hazel was still barred, yet Caz, the man responsible for Evie's pitiful condition, as the staff must know, was apparently allowed unrestricted access. It made no sense. It defied reason.

'Unsettling' might have been Professor Wainwright's word for Caz's visit, but Tarn could think of so many others that were far more apposite. 'Cruel' for one, she told herself as her taxi moved off. 'Monstrous' for another. And, ahead of them all, 'Unforgivable'.

Because that changed everything. It had to.

I was going to leave her, she castigated herself, gazing at the passing hedgerows with eyes that saw nothing. Abandon her to the mercy of someone who plays games with women's hearts and minds in order to save myself.

But she's not a survivor as past events have proved. And I am. So I'm going to stay and keep my promise, no matter what the cost. There'll be no unfinished business on my watch.

'My mother sends her love,' Della announced exuberantly as she tucked into the quiche. 'Also a Dundee cake, which we could have for afters.'

'Your mother's a saint.'

Della gave her a shrewd look. 'And how are your equally sanctified relatives?' she queried. 'I ask because you're looking a little worn round the edges, my pet.'

'Nonsense.' Tarn managed an approximation of a cheerful grin. 'All's well.' She'd already decided to say nothing about the day's revelations, telling herself it would solve no useful purpose.

'If you say so.' Della took more salad. 'And the publishing tycoon? Seen much of him lately?'

'Why, yes,' Tarn said lightly. 'We drove down to the coast yesterday.'

'Indeed?' Della raised her eyebrows. 'Well, I can only hope you know what you're doing.'

'Oh, I do,' Tarn said with quiet emphasis. 'I've never been so sure of anything in my life.'

'Fine,' Della said equably. 'Then there's no need for me to remind you of the old saying that it's much easier to ride a tiger than it is to dismount?'

'None at all.'

'Then I won't mention it.' She waved a fork. 'The cake, by the way, is in that tin over there.'

They spent a companionable evening watching television and chatting on a variety of deliberately non-taboo subjects, but Tarn was conscious there was a distance between them and regretted it.

But Evie had to matter more, she told herself.

She went to work as usual the next day, but just before noon complained of a severe headache and said she was going home to drawn curtains and painkillers.

She arrived at The Refuge prepared to do battle, but it was unnecessary. The nurse she had met previously took her straight to Evie's room.

'How is she?' Tarn asked, and the other woman pulled a face.

'Yesterday did her no good at all, but it couldn't

be avoided, and it probably won't be the last time. But it may cheer her up to see a friendly face.'

Evie was crouched in her chair, wan and red-eyed, nursing a box of tissues.

'Tarn.' She straightened. 'Oh, Tarn, it's been so awful. I'm so scared. You have to do something. You have to keep him away from me.'

'Yes.' Tarn pulled the other chair up beside her, and sat, taking her hand. 'I'll do my best, I promise, so try not to think about it. About him.'

'I thought I was safe here.' Evie swallowed. 'That he wouldn't know where I was.' Her voice rose slightly. 'I wasn't going to tell anyone about him—what he did. Truly I wasn't. He ought to know that. He seemed so kind, as if he wanted to look after me. I never realised what he was really like.'

'No, of course not,' Tarn said gently. 'Why should you?'

After all, I knew, she thought, and it made no difference. I still wanted him in spite of everything. So how can I blame you when I really ought to be disgusted with myself?

Tarn dragged herself back to the here and now. 'Evie—what actually happened yesterday? What was said?'

'I can't talk about it. I'm not allowed to. And,

anyway, I'm sick of questions. I won't answer any more.' She began to cry weakly. 'I just want to get out of here. I know I've been a fool, but I don't see why I should go on being punished like this. You have to do something, Tarn. You have to take me home.'

Easier said than done, Tarn thought as she sat on the train back to London. Evie had continued in much the same vein for the entire visit, alternating recrimination with bouts of self-pity. Tarn had done her best to make her think more positively about the future, talking of new jobs and a possible holiday in the sun, and being careful not to mention Caz by name, but her foster sister had just stared at her, wounded, and told her she didn't understand.

It was almost a relief when the nurse appeared and said that visiting time was up.

'I'll deal with him, Evie,' Tarn said softly, as she rose to her feet. 'When I've finished, he won't bother you again.'

'And tell them I won't answer any more questions,' Evie called after her, her voice sullen.

I won't be telling 'them' anything, thought Tarn. Whoever 'they' were.

She sighed to herself. If she was honest, she could see no prospect of an early release for Evie.

From what the younger girl had said, she was still confined to her room. Yet the other residents seemed to move round the house and gardens easily enough, under the watchful eyes of the staff, and the big board in the hall was crammed with notices about the various activity groups on offer. Surely joining with other people and finding new interests would contribute towards Evie's rehabilitation.

Whereas being made to confront her erstwhile fiancé would not. Especially as it seemed he might be exerting pressure on her to keep quiet about their relationship. And what were these so-called experts like the Professor thinking of to allow it?

Couldn't Caz see the state she was in? Tarn railed inwardly. Did he truly have no compassion or sense of guilt over the havoc he'd created in the life of someone who'd simply been too trusting and gullible for her own good?

And how, she asked herself almost helplessly, is it possible for him to be so different with me? Unless, of course, he's simply biding his time. Waiting until he's tired of me too.

And felt her whole body clench, as if warding off unbearable pain.

As she walked into the flat, the telephone was ringing.

'I heard you'd gone home sick,' Caz said. 'I was worried.'

Tarn took a deep breath. Steadied her voice. 'It was just a headache. It's gone now.'

'Then would you be free for dinner tonight—if I promise not to mention anything stressful?' There was a smile in his voice.

Tarn had the strange sensation that she was teetering on the edge of an abyss.

But it's not too late, she told herself desperately. Even now she could save herself. Step back to safety or...

Instead, she heard herself say huskily, 'I'd love to have dinner with you, Caz. And we can talk about anything you want.'

And threw herself into the waiting void.

CHAPTER NINE

HE TOOK her to the Trattoria Giuliana, as he said, 'For old times' sake.' They even had the same table as before.

As they sat down, he looked at her, his smile faintly rueful. 'Or am I being overly sentimental?'

'No,' she said. 'It's a lovely idea. I always hoped we'd come back here sometime.'

'Then why not make it a regular date,' he said, the hazel eyes caressing her. 'For the rest of our lives.' Then checked. 'But perhaps I'm being too optimistic. After all, I haven't had your answer yet.'

Tarn stared down at the tablecloth. 'I think you know what I'm going to say already.' And wondered how she could possibly sound so quiet and steady with the maelstrom of emotions raging within her.

'Or else you wouldn't be with me tonight?'

'Maybe,' she said. 'But I suppose I could be coy, and say I was still making up my mind.'

'You could.' His hand reached for hers across the table. 'But you won't. Will you?'

'No,' she said. 'I won't.' In spite of herself, the warm clasp of his fingers round hers was sending tendrils of sensation throughout her entire being. She paused, looking at him, and allowing her lips to part a little as if she was breathless. Except, she realised with shame, she did not have to pretend, because his lightest touch could do that to her. 'I—I will marry you, Caz. If you still want me.'

He said softly, 'More than I've ever wanted anything, my darling.' He signalled, and a beaming waiter arrived with champagne.

'My goodness.' She managed a laugh. 'You really were sure of yourself.'

'Not in the slightest.' He studied her for a moment, his expression quizzical. 'There's an elusiveness about you, Tarn. As I've said, I sensed it from the beginning. I'm wondering if it might not be wise to chain you to my wrist until we're safely married.'

He was too damned perceptive by half, Tarn thought. She raised her eyebrows. 'You regard marriage as safety? I thought it was an act of faith—a step into the dark.'

'Not for us.' He raised his glass. 'Here's to forever.'

He sounded so certain—so bloody sincere, she told herself as she responded to the toast and sipped her champagne. A man any girl would be glad to trust with her future. Unless, of course, she had the memory of Evie, cowering in her chair, to warn her and harden her heart against him. And she would need that every hour of every day.

Caz reached into an inside pocket and produced a small velvet box. He said, 'At the risk of seeming presumptuous, I brought you this.'

As he opened it, Tarn stiffened, expecting to be dazzled by another showy blaze of diamonds. But she was wrong. The diamonds in this ring were gleaming in discreet brilliance around an exquisite square sapphire in an antique gold setting.

The gasp that escaped her was of genuine wonder and delight. 'Oh—it's beautiful.'

'I'd hoped you'd like it,' he said. 'It's been in the family for a long time, and my grandmother gave it to me for this very occasion. It might have to be made smaller, of course. You have very slim hands.'

'No,' she said, dry-mouthed as he slid the ring on to her finger. 'It—it's quite perfect.'

'You're absolutely sure? It occurred to me you might prefer to keep this as a dress ring and have something modern for our engagement—a special design, maybe.'

She covered it protectively with her other hand. 'You couldn't give me anything lovelier.' Her response was instinctive—genuine. Because this could—should have been the happiest moment of her life, she thought with bewilderment. Yet, instead, she felt as if she was dying inside.

Judas, she said silently, *reborn as a woman.*

She took a deep breath. 'But I can't wear it, Caz. Not yet. Not in public.'

His brows snapped together in a frown. 'What are you talking about? Why the hell not?'

'Because I have a job to do,' she said steadily. 'Working for you in a section of one of your companies. That means a lot to me, and I don't want it to change, and it will, once word gets out about us.'

She forced a smile. 'Besides, when the news does break, it's bound to be a nine-day wonder, and I'm not sure I'm totally prepared for that. The fuss—the attention—stories in the papers. That's a lot to take on board—for me. So, can't we keep it as our secret—just for a while?'

'Now there we differ,' he said gently. 'Because I want to shout it from the rooftops. Tell the whole world what a lucky bastard I am.'

Tarn said with constraint, 'Are you certain that's what the whole world wants to hear?'

'Ah,' he said. 'I suppose we're back to Ginny again.' He took her hand again. 'My darling, the past doesn't matter.' His voice was warm and urgent. 'We can't let it—not when we have the future.'

And Evie? If she's part of your immaterial past too, why are you still harassing her? Why can't you leave her alone?

Now, if ever, was the time to ask these things. To come at him like a bolt from the blue and shock him, perhaps, into honesty. Even into contrition.

Before she walked away...

So why was she hesitating?

After all, she wanted to humiliate him. To let him know at first hand what it was like to be made a fool of and dumped. But a half-full restaurant on a Monday evening was not the public arena for the major victory she'd envisaged.

Better to bide her time, she thought, her throat tightening. Wait for the right moment and the maximum impact.

He said, 'You're doing it again, my love. Disappearing into some world where I can't follow.'

'Not really,' she said lightly, and paused. 'It's just that there's suddenly a lot to think about.'

'Then maybe we should start sharing some thoughts now,' he said. 'Do you want a big wedding?'

'Oh, no.' The negation was involuntary, and she'd have said exactly the same if this had been the beginning of their future, and the ceremony was to be a reality.

'You're very sure,' he commented, with faint amusement. 'I thought all women dreamed of floating down the aisle, wearing the obligatory meringue, in a country church crammed with well-wishers.'

Tarn wrinkled her nose. 'That's part of the problem. I'd have difficulty filling a pew.'

Caz pulled a face. 'And I know far too many people who would expect to be there, whether we wanted them or not,' he said. 'And someone I do want who, sadly, can't be there. So, why don't we do it quietly at a friendly neighbourhood register office? Will your cousin be well enough to act as one of the witnesses?'

Her heart skipped a beat. 'Well—no. At least she's not around,' she added hurriedly. 'She's gone away to convalesce. She needs absolute quiet, so she'll be gone for some time.'

Which at least was the truth.

'Your flatmate?'

She shook her head. 'She's away a lot. I'm not sure of her plans.'

'I see.' Caz was silent for a moment. 'Well, we could ask Brendan and Grace instead. I think you liked them when you met.'

'Yes,' said Tarn, despising herself for her faint feeling of desolation. 'Yes, I did.'

'And when the news of the wedding does get out, we shall have left on our honeymoon,' he went on. 'So we shall miss all the razzmatazz. And by the time we come back, everyone will be used to the idea. So it's a win-win situation for us.'

No, she thought. It will be a very different kind of victory. And you will be the loser. But she had no sense of triumph. Instead she felt as if every-thing within her had become a cold, aching hol-low.

The food and wine were delicious, but, for Tarn, they might have been bread and water. Her en-ergy and attention were fixed, as they had to be, on this new role she had to play—the happy and loving fiancée.

And, of course, on never letting herself forget that it was just a role. That it could never be any-thing else no matter what she might want or feel in her inmost being.

Because all that had to be suppressed. Pushed

out of sight, and eventually—please, God—out of mind. No more walking round the flat with her arms wrapped round her body, damming back the pain. No more tears, even if she could manage to weep silently.

He said, 'You're very quiet,' and she looked at him, startled.

'I think I'm just stunned.' She made herself smile. 'It's been a hell of a forty-eight hours, and it takes some getting used to.'

'For me too, believe it or not.' He paused. 'What we need is some time alone and in private. Let's get out of here and have our coffee elsewhere.'

'But Della's at the flat...'

'Darling, I meant my place, not yours.' He smiled at her. 'Besides, it will give you the chance to have a good look round and tell me what you'd like to change.'

'Change?'

And I have seen it—all of it—the other night. And imagined you there with Evie...

'Of course. You're bound to have some ideas about your future home.' His grin was teasing. 'I'd be disappointed if you didn't.'

'Your flat,' Tarn said slowly. 'You'd want us to live there. I—I didn't realise.' One of many things she hadn't taken into account, she thought. The way he already had their lives mapped out in this straight and shining path. But she couldn't turn back now. She had to go on. Had to…

'I thought—to begin with at least,' he said. 'While we decide where and what our permanent home should be.' He gave her a searching look. 'You're not keen?'

'I hardly know.' She searched for an excuse. 'It's just that everything's moving so fast…'

'Not for me,' Caz said softly. 'Given the chance, I'd get a special licence and carry you off this week.'

She forced a smile. 'I think you'll have to be patient with me.'

'I can do patient.' His tone was rueful. 'Although I may struggle a bit.' He took her hand again. 'You'll have to make allowances too, my sweet. Promise?'

'Yes,' Tarn said and hated herself.

She stood in the centre of that vast living room, trying not to shiver as Caz took her wrap from her shoulders and tossed it over the arm of a sofa before discarding his own jacket.

'What do you want to see first?' His voice was teasing. 'The kitchen? After all, there's coffee to be made.'

She eased away from him. 'I think you can manage that perfectly well without my interference.'

'Then start the tour without me.' He slanted a grin at her as he headed off. 'I'll be asking questions later.'

She'd noticed the big vibrant canvases that hung on the pale walls during her previous visit, but tonight there were no friends or caterers to provide a distraction—or to act as a barrier, said a warning voice in her head—so she had time to look around properly—examine the pictures at her leisure.

Like Evie, she was no expert, but she could see they deserved attention, their colours and textures drawing the eye and invading the imagination, their effect enhanced by careful lighting.

But there were other, homelier touches too. She noticed some charming ceramics, not old enough to be valuable, on a table and walked over to look at a group of photographs on top of a bookcase. Her gaze travelled from a couple, not young, standing smiling in the sunlight in front of a wall, draped in wisteria, to some children on a beach with a black Labrador, and, lastly, standing by an elegant fireplace, an elderly woman whose white hair belied the command of a strong but beautiful face.

Looking down at the sapphire ring, Tarn wondered if this was the grandmother who'd planned for his marriage.

I'm sorry. She sent the message out into the ether. I'm so sorry, and I'm glad you can't know what's going to happen.

When Caz returned with the coffee, she was standing at the window, staring at the lamplit panorama.

'At sunset, it's truly spectacular.' He set down the tray. 'Come and sit down. Can I offer you some brandy?'

'Better not.' She kept her tone light. 'My head's whirling quite enough, I think.'

She took her place next to him and accepted the cup he handed to her, breathing the coffee's rich, heady aroma.

She said, 'I've been admiring your pictures.' She paused, adding deliberately, 'You'll have to teach me what they're all about.'

He gave a rueful shrug. 'I have a mate called Adam who'd be a far better instructor. My choices are instinctive rather than informed, and he says I've been damned lucky not to have been taken for a ride so far. When you meet him, ask him anything you want to know.'

'But I understood you were a connoisseur.' She could not hide her surprise.

Caz's mouth twisted. 'Well, I can't imagine where you heard that, flattering though it may be.' He added, 'And I hope you're not disappointed, now you know the truth.'

'No,' she said quickly. 'Not a bit. Besides, your method is probably better than picking something that ticks a lot of boxes with art critics. And I'd rather hear why you chose them.'

'Let's save that for some long winter evening,' he suggested softly. 'We have other things to discuss tonight.'

Her heartbeat quickened. 'Yes—of course.'

'For one thing, you need to see the rest of the place, including the kitchen, even if I couldn't tempt you in there just now.' He paused, putting down his cup. 'My God,' he said. 'I never thought to ask. You can cook, I suppose.'

'Now there's a male chauvinist question.' Her glance held mock reproof. 'If I say no, will you want your ring back?'

'Far from it,' Caz said cheerfully. 'I'm not looking for a domestic slave. If necessary, I'll simply get the meals myself.' He paused. 'But I admit it would be nicer if it was a joint affair.'

'Much nicer,' she said. 'And I may as well confess right now that I love cooking.'

'Excellent.' He took her cup from her hand and set it down, then moved closer, sliding his arms round her and pulling her against him. 'And as love has been mentioned,' he murmured. 'Now might also be a good time for you to tell me how you feel about me.'

'I thought I'd already made that clear.' Her voice shook a little as the warmth of him, the scent of his skin began at once to work their dark, insidious magic.

'All the same, my darling, I need to hear you say it.' He pushed back her hair from her face, letting his lips graze her temple. 'Would it be so very difficult?'

You don't know. Oh, God, you just don't know...

But at least, for once, she could speak the truth without evasion.

For this moment, she thought, just for this moment.

She said quietly, 'I love you, Caz. I think I did from the first, only I couldn't—I didn't want to admit it when there were so many reasons not to. So many reasons for me to keep my distance.

'But now it's said and I can tell you that I shall go on loving you for the rest of my life.'

The truth, the whole truth and nothing but the truth...

Heaven help me, she thought.

He said hoarsely, 'Oh, God, Tarn, my sweet, wonderful girl.'

He began to kiss her, gently at first, then with increased passion, his mouth moving on hers in urgent sensuous demand.

And Tarn responded, eagerly, helplessly, her arms around his neck, her breasts crushed against his chest, as her lips parted for him.

Just for this moment.

A moment when nothing else in the world existed but the sweet draining delight of his kisses. She found herself sighing her pleasure into his mouth, arching towards him as she felt the first heated explicit thrust of his tongue and offered him an equally candid response in her turn, clinging to him, drinking from the shared moisture of their mouths.

She smiled as she experienced the warmth of his lips caressing her closed eyes, the curve of her cheek, and the crazy throb of the pulse in her throat.

Caz pushed her back against the softness of the cushions, his hands moving slowly but very surely, skimming the delicate line of her shoulders, then sliding down to cup her breasts and stroke them gently through the silky top she was wearing, coaxing her nipples to rise to hard, aching peaks under the passionate certainty of his touch.

Tarn gasped, her head thrown back, her whole being consumed by the long, delicious shivers that were running through her, inspiring her to let her fingers in their turn begin their own exploration—discover the taut muscularity of his back and trace the long supple spine through his fine linen shirt.

To feel the heat of his body as it pressed on hers, and find it echoed in the giddy rush of her own blood stream, and in the deep, inner trembling of her ungiven flesh as she encountered the hardness of his arousal against her slender thighs.

The thin layers of cloth that separated them seemed suddenly too great a barrier. With a kind of desperation, Tarn wanted to be naked in his arms. Naked with him. To find herself at last possessed and know the rapture of his body sheathed in hers.

To understand why she had made herself wait all this time.

Just for this moment. Just for this man. Whom she could not have...

He was kissing her again, slowly, deeply, and she cried out softly in longing and despair, her voice breaking as she whispered his name against his mouth.

'My angel.' His voice was hoarse, his hand heavy on her bare thigh where he'd pushed her skirt aside. 'Tarn—stay with me tonight, darling—please. Give yourself to me.'

All she need do was remain silent and he would lift her and carry her to his room. And to the bed he'd shared with Evie...

It was that realisation that, somehow, forced her to clutch at her reeling sanity. Made her find the words that would save her. 'I—I can't.' She stared up into his eyes, lambent with desire. 'You—you said you wouldn't pressure me. You promised...'

'I did,' Caz said quietly after a pause. 'And I meant it. But I'm only human, my sweet, so you can't blame me for trying.' He sat up, pushing his hair back from his sweat-dampened forehead while Tarn ordered her dishevelled clothing with unsteady hands.

She said, stumbling a little, 'Are you angry with me?'

'No,' he said gently. 'Why would I be? I want you very much, Tarn, but it has to be mutual.' He added ruefully, 'And for a few moments there, I thought it was.'

'It was.' Her voice shook. 'It is. You must believe that.' She hesitated. 'It's just—being here—in your flat. I don't know how to explain.' She swallowed. 'I can only say that it has—connections that I can't forget—and never will.'

Ask me, she thought. Ask me exactly what I mean and I'll tell you, so that I can put a stop to the whole thing once and for all. Because I can't bear to go on like this. It's ripping me in pieces.

'Ah.' He was silent for a moment, then sighed. 'I must be extraordinarily insensitive, my darling, because it truly never occurred to me that my bachelor indiscretions would come back to haunt me in this particular way.'

He took her back into his arms. 'But if that's how you feel, so be it.' His lips brushed her hair. 'You don't have to live here, sweetheart, or even spend one solitary night with me. I'll put this place on the market, and we'll find somewhere else—somewhere new, with no connotations from the past whatsoever. We can start looking this week.'

'You'd do that for me?' She turned her face into his shoulder.

'That and far more,' he said. 'How many times must I say it?' He paused. 'Tarn, I wish I knew what had happened in your life to make you so reluctant to trust me. Will you tell me—one day?'

'Yes.' Her voice was muffled. She was thankful she didn't have to look into his eyes. 'Yes—one day.'

When Tarn got back to the flat, she found Della curled up on the living room sofa in her dressing gown.

'Oh, hi.' Tarn checked in surprise. 'I thought you'd be asleep.'

'No.' Della rose to her feet. 'I had things on my mind, and I wanted to talk to you.' She took a breath. 'Tarn, are you engaged to Caspar Brandon?'

Tarn's lips parted in a gasp of shock. But she can't know that, she thought. Not possibly.

She said with perfect truth, 'I—I don't understand.'

'Nor do I—but I found this.' Della produced Evie's ring box from her pocket. 'It was on the sideboard and—well, I'm afraid I had a look inside. I had no right to do that, and you've every reason to be angry with me.

'But I want you to know that whatever you've said about him—everything you've believed is absolutely true. He is a love rat and a cheat, and this proves it. So please tell me that if you are engaged to him, it's for you own purposes and not because you've also been taken in by his charm and his lies.'

'Dell, slow down.' Tarn's head was whirling. 'What on earth are you talking about? That's Evie's engagement ring. Her diamonds, not mine.'

Della snorted. 'Diamonds be damned. They're cubic zirconia. Pretty to look at but worth a fraction of the real thing.' She shook her head. 'I admit I had my doubts about Evie because I've always considered her a total flake. But Caz Brandon is far worse. A bigger fake than his so-called diamonds.'

She sighed before continuing. 'I know I was against what you were planning, but you were right, and I was wrong. He dazzled that poor silly girl into his bed and dumped her when he was tired of her. And I've discovered something else. That place she's been locked up in—well, he's on the board of trustees. That's why it's so difficult for you to see her and talk to her. Because he put her there, conveniently out of his way.'

Tarn stared at her, the beat of her heart slamming slowly and heavily against her ribcage. She said in a whisper, 'Are you—quite sure?'

'I looked him up on line—not the social stuff—

but the directorships and other connections outside his publishing empire, and found it. Then I checked back with The Refuge to make sure. Not just a trustee but listed as a benefactor. With his sort of money, you can get away with anything.'

Della took a deep breath. 'But I'm here now to say that he deserves everything that's coming to him, and if I can help you bring him down, I will.'

Tarn took the little box from her outstretched hand and opened it slowly, staring down at the icy glitter of the stones. Wondering how she could have been so deceived. Why she too hadn't recognised at once that they were not real diamonds.

But nothing about his relationship with Evie had been true, she thought. And he dared ask me to trust him…

Pain twisted to agony inside her as she re-lived the memory of being in his arms. He chooses his bait according to his victim, she thought. With Evie, it was all glamour and the high life. But with me, it was sex.

And I so nearly fell for it—for all the well-worn technique he's practised over the years. How could I have been so weak—so stupid?

She said, her voice harsh, 'I disliked this ring from the moment I saw it. It was too big, too showy, but I told myself that at least it seemed to prove that he'd really cared for her once.

'And even though I was wrong about that, I'll make sure that he cares eventually. That he'll regret to his dying day what he did to Evie.'

And for myself, she added silently. How much will I be left to regret—and for how long?

And knew that, in spite of everything, her regrets could last for the rest of her life.

CHAPTER TEN

THINGS, Tarn told herself, were moving altogether too far and too fast, as if she was a novice skier caught heading downwards on a black run.

Her first shock had been the sale of Caz's flat less than a week after it had gone on the market.

'There were four offers,' he told her that evening, with a tinge of ruefulness. 'Even the agents were surprised.'

'Well—it's a beautiful flat,' Tarn returned, glancing around her, and suppressing a slight pang of her own.

But she couldn't weaken now, she thought. He deserved to lose it. To know what it was like to be left with nothing.

'But sadly not beautiful enough to tempt you to forget my bachelor sins and stay here.' Caz lifted her on to his knee and held her close, his lips against her hair. 'Now we have to find somewhere for ourselves alone.'

The next shock had been to find herself being

escorted round a whole series of the kind of properties she'd only ever imagined in her dreams and having constantly to remind herself that dreams were all they could remain.

She'd envisaged Caz becoming bored and possibly irritated at being involved in an endless quest which he must regard as unnecessary, but, however contrary her behaviour, and she remained consistently hard to please, his patience and good humour remained constant.

And their shared sense of the ridiculous provided her with some awkward moments when his sardonic sideways glance when the agent was happily eulogising some terrible interior design excess almost reduced her to helpless giggles.

'It's lovely,' Tarn admitted, after they'd left yet another glamorous penthouse and returned to Caz's flat. 'But it's just a showcase. I bet no-one's so much as chopped an onion in that kitchen. And do we really need a hot tub in the roof garden?'

Caz took her in his arms and kissed her slowly and thoroughly. 'A shower big enough to share is quite enough for me,' he whispered. 'Maybe we should ruin the Realtor's day and ask to see rather simpler properties from now on.' He gave her a long look. 'And the sooner the better. You're beginning to look a little tense, my sweet. Is the pre-wedding pressure getting to you?'

If he only knew, thought Tarn, remembering the nights when she'd walked the floor unable to sleep, her mind trying feverishly to detach itself from recent memories of sitting curled up beside him on the sofa, watching television or listening to music together.

Reminding herself that none of it was real, except, perhaps, her involuntary response to the tender restraint of his lovemaking, the gentle arousal of his hands and mouth on her body which was all he would allow himself just before he took her home.

And that, to her shame, was where pretence stopped.

She forced a smile. 'Hardly. After all, we haven't actually set a date yet.'

'Something else we need to remedy.' He paused. 'Do you still want to keep our engagement a deadly secret, or shall we say "To hell with it" and surprise the world with an announcement in The Times?'

Tarn hesitated. She'd been wondering how to introduce the subject, and now he'd done it for her. Her chance had come, and she had to take it.

Now, she thought, or never.

She said, trying to sound casual. 'Actually, the garden party's next week. I was thinking we might go public then. That is—if you agree.'

Caz's brows lifted. 'I'd be delighted.' His tone was faintly quizzical. 'But are you sure?'

She shrugged lightly. 'Let's just say I'm becoming used to the idea.' She paused. 'Of course, I'll have to hand in my notice at work. I don't want to be regarded as a boardroom spy.'

'That's a pity,' he said quietly. 'When you're so good at your job. Won't you miss it?'

'Yes, but I'll have plenty of other things to occupy me.' Meaning, she thought edgily, the growing list of potential projects from her British and American agents, about which she would soon have to make some definite decisions.

Her Chameleon camouflage was right there, waiting for her to slip back into it as if nothing had happened and she'd never been away. And she should be feeling grateful for that, she told herself fiercely, instead of suddenly cold and bleak.

'So,' Della said when Tarn got home. 'Have you put a down payment yet on your future love nest? Or are you still prevaricating over these multi-million pads he keeps trotting out for your inspection?'

'Still managing to keep the whole issue at bay.' Tarn accepted the cup of coffee Della handed her.

'But for how much longer? Or are you planning for him to become homeless and be forced to occupy a cardboard box in some alleyway?'

'There's no chance of that.' Tarn sat down on the sofa as if her legs were too weary to support her any longer. 'Besides, the sale hasn't been completed on his present flat. He can always pull out.'

'True.' Della nodded. 'On the other hand, honey, if you're too choosy, he might begin to smell a rat.'

'He won't have time,' Tarn said harshly. 'He's going to announce our engagement in front of everyone at the company garden party next week, and that will be closely followed by my own special announcement. End of story.'

'Wow.' Della whistled. 'Short and extremely sharp. In other circumstances, I could almost feel sorry for him.' She paused. 'Have you told Evie what you're planning?'

Tarn shook her head. 'I haven't had the chance. She's strictly incommunicado again for some unknown reason. No doubt on my fiancé's orders,' she added jerkily. 'But I'll tell her when it's done, and before I leave. At least that beastly professor can hardly stop me from saying goodbye to her.'

'The whole place needs exposing,' said Della.

'One of the PAs at work has a cousin who's an investigative journalist. He might be interested.'

'A good idea, but I'd like to be out of the way first.' Her coffee tasted unusually bitter and Tarn put her cup down, unfinished, knowing it was not down to the brew but rather the fault of the nerves twisting in her stomach.

Nerves which Caz, of course, had noticed...

But I mustn't arouse his suspicions, she thought. Not at this late stage. Because nothing can go wrong now. I won't let it.

Tarn opened her eyes on the Saturday of the garden party to find bright sunlight streaming through the curtains. Clearly her waking dream that the whole event had been washed out by flash floods would not be coming true, she thought as she pushed the coverlet away and got reluctantly out of bed.

The dress she'd bought a few days earlier was hanging on the front of her wardrobe, cool and simple in white lawn with self-embroidery at the scoop-neck and around the hem of the full skirt.

'Bridal white, eh?' Della had asked, lifting her eyebrows when she saw it. 'Just to rub more salt into the wound, I suppose.'

'Actually no,' Tarn returned, a mite defensively. 'I just thought it looked pretty and summery.'

Looking at it now, however, she had to acknowledge that it could easily have been chosen as a dress for a very quiet wedding, perhaps with a small bouquet of pink roses. And stopped there, jolted by the path her thoughts had taken.

Out of the realms of fancy and down to earth, she scolded herself as she showered. She could have done with a pep talk from Della right now, but the other girl had been called away by her boss on a sales trip, standing in for a sick colleague.

So Tarn had been forced to make do with her erstwhile flatmate's warm hug and a fierce 'Good luck—and I'll be seeing you.'

Although it was not certain when that would be, she mused. Probably not for a considerable while, as she had tracks to cover. But Della fully understood that.

She towelled herself briskly and put on her underwear, then used a hand dryer to encourage her hair into its usual gleaming waves before donning mundane jeans and a T-shirt.

The rest of her clothes were already packed, and when the afternoon was over, and she'd paid her final visit to Evie, she would book in to some anonymous airport hotel until she could get a flight to the States.

She grilled bacon, scrambled a couple of eggs to go with it plus three slices of wholemeal toast. After all, there'd be no champagne buffet after she'd delivered her bombshell, so she probably wouldn't get another full meal until sometime in the evening, and she needed to keep her energy levels up for the task ahead of her.

Besides, once it was over, she wasn't sure when she would feel like eating ever again. Even now, she was having to force the food down into her churning stomach.

When she'd finished and cleared away, she went to her laptop to see what late deals there might be in hotel rooms, and found to her surprise that there was an item of mail waiting for her. From Caz.

She hadn't expected to hear from him. Unless, she thought, he was making a last attempt to persuade her to travel down to Winsleigh Place with him, instead of taking the coach with her colleagues.

She clicked on to his message, then sat, stunned, staring blankly at the few, hasty lines on the screen sent from his iPhone.

'Sweetheart,' hc wrote. 'Something's come up

and sadly I can't make it to the party. Have a great time yourself and I'll call you as soon as I get back.'

She said, 'No.' Then repeated it, 'No, no, *no*,' more violently each time, banging her fist on the table as she saw her great plan shatter into fragments around her.

The sleepless nights, she thought dazedly. The days of tension, always struggling against self-betrayal. The constant rehearsing of what she intended to say until she was word-perfect. And, more than anything, the pain of steeling herself against the moment when she would turn her back and walk away from him forever.

All of it for nothing.

She looked at her waiting travel bags. If she'd ever been the superstitious kind, she could tell herself it was a sign, cut her losses and run.

And paused right there, looking back at the screen. Reading his message again.

Because, she realised, there was, of course, another explanation. A totally different sign for her to ponder.

She had to face the fact that Caz had indeed been operating the same kind of pretence with her as he had with Evie, but was now bored with that too, and bringing the interlude to a close.

After all, Tarn thought, biting her lip until she tasted blood, he didn't fight too much when I asked to keep our engagement a secret, so perhaps that suited his purposes just as well as mine. And I was too taken up with my own plans to see it.

Besides, he doesn't have much to show for the past weeks of intensive courtship. He hasn't even succeeded in seducing me, unlike poor Evie, and now the deadline for losing his beloved flat is approaching. Maybe that's what's prompted him into thinking that the game isn't worth the candle and made him decide to walk away.

Because a public announcement in front of his workforce had turned out to be a step too far, even for him.

She felt deathly cold. She'd known from the start that it was a possibility, even a probability that he chose his women in much the same way as he'd purchase a new silk tie, and would subsequently discard them once their novelty value had dissipated.

Quite apart from Evie, the example of Ginny Fraser should have taught her that. Because she was in the past. He'd said so quite unequivocally, from the stance of a man who did not look back.

Oh, God, hadn't she told herself over and over again that falling in love with him was a weakness she couldn't afford. While believing, even for a moment, that he loved her in return was sheer madness.

The wishful thinking of a relatively inexperienced girl, beguiled beyond reason by an all-too-experienced man. Tempted out of her senses by the deceptive tenderness of his lovemaking.

How could I ever have pitied Evie, she thought, a faint moan rising in her throat, when the only difference between us is that he won't have to find a place for me in one of The Refuge's convenient recovery programmes?

Because I will survive this. I'll survive him.

And I shall be the one to walk away first.

But today, the only place I'm going is to a garden party. As arranged.

Winsleigh Place was just as beautiful as everyone had said. The house itself was Georgian, an elegant jewel in a magnificent setting.

'How on earth do we get to have a party in a place like this?' Tarn asked, turning to Lisa in disbelief as she surveyed the sculptured lawns, now dotted with colourful marquees, which led down to a small lake.

'As I said, we have Caz to thank,' Lisa said, shrugging. 'I gather there could be some distant family connection, or maybe he just has influence in high places, but no-one is really sure.'

'No,' Tarn said lightly. 'Probably not.'

'Pity he can't be here himself,' Lisa went on. 'Rumour has it that he's in France. One of the Parisian directors seems to be the world's most difficult man and Caz is always having to dash over and sort things out, usually to prevent some kind of mass walk-out. I guess history has re-peated itself this weekend.'

'Perhaps.' Tarn shrugged. 'Whatever the reason, he's missing a treat, even if he did organise it.'

In one corner, a stage had been erected under a striped awning and here a jazz band was playing. Elsewhere there were old-fashioned sports like skittles, quoits, and even a coconut shy, while in another part of the garden a croquet tournament was taking place.

'There's a fortune teller too.' Lisa pointed to a brightly painted bow-topped vardo. 'Fancy a glimpse into the future?'

'I don't think so.' Tarn's smile was taut. 'She'd probably tell me I was going to meet a tall, dark stranger.'

'And that's bad?'

'It could be. Anyway, I'm not going to risk it.'

'Well, I have to look out for my own tall, dark

stranger.' Lisa patted her arm. 'He was taking the children for lunch at my mother's first.' She paused. 'I have to say, Tarn, that you look absolutely amazing. I love that dress, and I find it astonishing that you haven't been snapped by some lucky guy long before this.'

Her smile was mischievous. 'On the other hand, maybe you'll have your encounter with destiny right here—even without the gipsy's warning.'

Left to herself, Tarn wandered across the grass, moving between the groups of laughing, chattering people, exchanging smiles and greetings with those she knew, and realising ruefully how comparatively few of them there were. And this was only a small section of the Brandon empire.

'It is Tarn, isn't it?'

She turned in surprise to see an older woman, in a dark blue linen dress, her blonde hair in an immaculate chignon, whom she recognised as Caz's principal PA, until now only seen from a distance in the office.

'Oh.' She hesitated. 'Good afternoon, Mrs Everett.'

'Make it Maggie, please.' The other's smile was relaxed and friendly. 'I was sure it must be you. I told myself there couldn't be two people in the UK company with quite that glorious shade of hair.'

Tarn flushed. 'Well—thank you.'

'Caz asked me to look out for you,' Maggie Everett went on and Tarn froze.

'He did?' she managed feebly.

'Why, yes. In his unavoidable absence, I have strict instructions to make sure you have plenty of champagne. Although there are loads of iced soft drinks, if you prefer.'

She was steering Tarn towards the largest marquee. And as there was no longer any need to keep a clear head, Tarn decided that champagne it should be.

Mrs Everett, whose husband, she told Tarn, was a successful barrister who believed that wives should pursue their own careers if they wished, proved an amazingly easy companion for someone who was dubbed Caz's Rottweiler by a number of the Brandon workforce.

Tarn couldn't figure afterwards whether it was the other woman's friendliness, her own emotional turmoil or the potent effect of a vintage wine that made her reckless, only that during a lull in the conversation, she found herself saying, 'I knew someone who used to work at Brandon a few months ago. Do you remember Eve Griffiths?'

Maggie Everett thought for a moment. 'The

name rings no bells, I'm afraid,' she said eventually. 'Which department was she in?'

'I believe she used to work for Mr Brandon himself.'

'I really don't think that can be possible.' Mrs Everett frowned a little. 'I know everyone who has worked for all the board members during the past year, even on a temporary basis, and there's certainly been no-one called Griffiths. Your friend must have been employed elsewhere in the company.'

'Oh, she's hardly a friend,' Tarn said swiftly. 'Just—someone I met who said Brandon was a great company to work for. I probably assumed she worked for Caz—Mr Brandon, that is.'

Because that's what Evie said in all her letters, and I can't be wrong about it. I can't be...

Mrs Everett's grey eyes twinkled. 'There's no need to be so formal, I assure you, and certainly not with me. Anyway, relax—have some more champagne. You must be very disappointed that Caz can't be here,' she added. 'But I know it has to be for the very best of reasons.'

Whereas I, thought Tarn as her glass was refilled, no longer know what to think—about anything.

Wanting a quick change of subject, she said, 'That's a very good band.'

'All locals, who play here every year. But if you want a change of sound from Dixieland, there's a string quartet in the drawing room who special-ise in Mozart. And, of course, another band for tonight's dancing.'

'All tastes catered for,' Tarn commented lightly.

'Caz likes his staff to be happy,' Maggie Everett returned.

At least until they're surplus to his require-ments, thought Tarn. Thought it, but did not say it.

Her companion's mobile phone buzzed and she excused herself to answer it, moving away to a short distance.

When she came back, her eyes were dancing again. 'Shall we continue our stroll? See what else is going on?'

Probably wiser than staying where they were and consuming more champagne, Tarn thought ruefully as they emerged from the marquee. For a moment, she paused, dazzled by the sunlight, blinking as she reached hurriedly into her bag for her dark glasses because she was seeing things. She had to be, otherwise Caz was walking towards her across the lawn, smiling, and that couldn't be happening.

Because he couldn't make it. He'd said so, she thought, and only realised she'd spoken aloud when she heard Mrs Everett laugh softly.

'Nevertheless, here he is.' She gave Tarn a gentle nudge. 'Aren't you going to welcome him?'

Tarn took one faltering step, then another, still unable to credit that he was really here, believing it only when she found herself in his arms and held close while he kissed her.

'Surprised?' he whispered.

'Yes—yes, of course.' Her head was whirling. 'Someone said you were in France...'

'I was. That's where I called from. But the situation wasn't as bad as I thought so I got an air taxi back.' He let her go reluctantly. 'God, Maggie was right,' he said, his green gaze scanning her with delighted appreciation. 'She said you looked absolutely beautiful. But a bit forlorn too. She thought you were missing me.' He slid an arm round her waist and began to walk with her towards the band platform. 'I hope that's true. Still want to marry me?'

'Caz—I...'

'And the answer had better be yes,' he went on. 'Or I shall kiss you in front of all these people until it is. Now come on, sweetheart. We have news to break.'

The clarinettist stepped forward and helped Tarn up on to the stage while the trombonist handed Caz a microphone.

There was a pause while the trumpeter blew a ringing fanfare, then Caz spoke.

'First of all, I want to welcome you all here on this special afternoon.' His voice was clear and steady as people came forward, clustering round the edge of the stage. 'Many of you will already know Tarn as a colleague. However it's my great joy to be able to tell you that she'll soon be taking on another job—that of being my wife. We both wanted all of you here to be the first to know, although there will be a notice in The Times on Monday.'

Amid gasps and a ripple of cheering, he reached down and took the champagne flute that Maggie Everett handed him.

'So, I'd like you all to raise your glasses and drink to my adorable girl, the future Mrs Caz Brandon.'

The laughter and applause reached a crescendo, voices calling out, 'To Caz and Tarn. God bless them,' as the toast was honoured.

Caz took his grandmother's ring from his breast pocket and slipped it on to her finger. He said softly, 'Now it's there forever, my love,' and kissed her lightly and sensuously on the lips to even louder cheering.

Someone from the crowd who might have been Lisa shouted, 'Come on, Tarn. It's your turn. Speech.'

Caz handed her the mike. 'It's all yours, darling.'

Her fingers closed round it. She stared down at the sea of faces, all expectant, all smiling, and clearly all waiting for her to say—what? How happy she was? How much in love?

Yet somewhere in her brain, she knew, was a very different speech, one she had learned by heart for this actual moment.

So why couldn't she remember one word of it?

All she could think of was how her heart had lifted in a kind of astonished joy when she saw Caz coming towards her.

How she'd found herself thinking as she stood in stunned disbelief, He loves me. He must do. Why else would he have dashed back to be with me? To do this?

A realisation that had thrown reason and emotion back into the melting pot.

She tried to visualise Evie, small and hunched in her chair, but could see nothing but the way Caz's smile lit his eyes when he looked at her. As he was looking at her right then, drying her mouth and making her heart thud unevenly.

And she knew then and there that what she'd intended—how she'd planned the afternoon to end was now quite impossible, even if it was for all the wrong reasons.

Someone called out, 'A silent woman, boss. Aren't you a lucky man.'

And on the roar of laughter that followed, Tarn found her voice.

She said shakily, 'I can't think of anything to say except—thank you for sharing this wonderful moment with us. I—I shall never forget it.' She turned towards Caz. 'And neither, I'm sure, will my fiancé.'

Because it's not over yet, she told herself silently, as Caz took the hand that wore his ring and kissed it. It's merely postponed—to another time—another place.

And somehow—then—I'll find the strength and the will to go through with it at last.

CHAPTER ELEVEN

'BUT what happened?' asked Della.

Tarn shook her head. 'I don't know. It was the perfect opportunity, but—I—I couldn't say it.' She groaned. 'Not with everyone looking at me and smiling.'

'So what will you do at the wedding?' Della's tone was caustic. 'Take this man for your lawful wedded husband so that everyone continues to smile?'

Tarn flinched. She said in a low voice, 'There won't be any wedding. I admit that the date's been set and the register office booked, but that's where it will end.' She drew a deep breath. 'Everything I planned to say, I shall put in a letter to be delivered by courier just before the ceremony is due to take place.'

'I see.' Della was silent for a moment, then said more gently, 'Have you worked out why you don't want to confront him face to face?'

Tarn turned away. She said dully, 'Yes, I know.

And I can't—I dare not risk it.' She swallowed. 'When he said he wasn't going to be at the garden party, I really thought he was going to dump me, just as he'd done with Evie. But suddenly there he was, and I realised I'd misjudged him and I felt—well, that doesn't matter—but that was another reason why I couldn't do what I'd planned.'

'That's exactly what I was afraid of.' Della sighed. 'Oh, God, what an unholy mess. Didn't someone once say that revenge was a two-edged sword?' She paused. 'I have to say that's the most beautiful ring, and definitely the genuine article this time.'

'Yes.' Tarn bit her lip. 'It is—very lovely. It will be enclosed with the letter.'

'I suppose so.' Della hesitated. 'Did he say why he'd cried off from the party originally?'

'Some problem at the Paris office, I think. He was going to tell me about it, then someone else came up to congratulate us, and afterwards, he said that, on second thoughts, it would keep.'

'Always supposing he gets a second chance,' said Della. She paused. 'Have you told Evie yet what you're going to do?'

'I haven't had the chance.' Tarn pulled a face. 'I wanted to see her the day after the garden party, but my request was turned down. And I wanted to ask her about her time at Brandon, too.

'You see, she told me she worked for Caz, but Maggie Everett his chief PA has never heard of her.'

Della shrugged. 'She could be under strict orders from above.'

'But that could hardly be applied to the entire workforce,' Tarn argued. 'And the fact is that no-one remembers her working there, not even Tony Lee from the Art Department who makes a routine beeline for every pretty blonde.

'He says there was an Emma who was a temp in the Finance section around that time, but she was Australian and engaged to a rugby player, so he backed off. But no Eve, Evie and Evelyn anywhere.'

She frowned. 'Which just seems—odd. Because where could she have met Caz except at Brandon?'

'Honey, the oddities about Evie and her mother, come to that, would fill several pages of A4.' Della paused. 'But isn't talking openly about Evie something of a risk?'

'I doubt anyone's going to report me,' Tarn said drily. 'And, as I'm not on the payroll but just working a couple of days a week now to finalise a project, it's probably my last chance.'

'Did The Refuge offer any explanation for barring you yet again?' asked Della.

'No, and when I explained there was something I needed to ask her, the Professor said very curtly that she'd answered enough questions.' Tarn sighed. 'Heaven knows what that was supposed to mean.'

'Her mother might know.'

'Yes.' Tarn's voice was rueful. 'That's another visit I have to pay. Aunt Hazel still can't understand why I haven't waved my magic wand and got Evie out of "that awful place". And her last message was so garbled, I could only pick out that she wanted me to help with some enquiries.'

'Approaching her MP, perhaps,' Della suggested. 'I can imagine my mother's reaction if I was shut up somewhere and she wasn't allowed to see me. Especially if my ex-boyfriend was responsible,' she added darkly.

'Yes,' Tarn said wearily. 'I haven't forgotten that—even for a minute.'

It was something that haunted her continually— the strange dichotomy between Caz's ruthless treatment of Evie, and his entirely different behaviour to herself.

She'd walked round the gardens at Winsleigh Place, her hand in his, floating on a cloud of good wishes. And later, she'd danced the evening away in his arms like an enchanted princess with her prince, as if, for them, midnight would never strike.

But it had, and here she was once more, facing the harshness of reality.

'Are you meeting him later?' Della asked.

'Yes, we're going to look at another flat this evening. The agent says it's an older property that's been completely renovated, and it could be the blank canvas we're looking for.' She bent her head wretchedly. 'Oh, God, I'm such a hypocrite.'

'Caz Brandon, of course, being squeaky clean.' Della gave her a straight look. 'Knowing what he's capable of, could you ever truly trust him or be happy with him? Be honest.'

Tarn smiled unhappily. 'Then, in honesty, I can only say—I don't know.'

But the certainty she could not bear to contemplate, she thought, pain wrenching at her, was the misery that would be waiting for her when he was no longer part of her life.

And how soon that day was approaching.

* * *

'Well, you've taken your time,' was Aunt Hazel's greeting, her plump face set in martyred lines. 'I told you it was an emergency.'

Tarn bent to kiss her cheek. 'I came as soon as I could.' She kept her tone gentle. 'What do you want me to do?'

'I want you to find out what's going on.' Aunt Hazel spoke with energy. 'What the police are doing with my poor Evie. It's not a criminal offence to try to kill yourself—not any longer, so why is she being harassed like this? If they want to chase someone, it should be the brute who drove her to it, and you must tell them so.'

Tarn was startled. 'Evie's involved with the police? Surely not.'

Mrs Griffiths nodded. 'Helping them with their enquiries, which is what they always say.' She snorted. 'Her father must be turning in his grave at the very idea.'

'But there must be some mistake...' Tarn began, but was testily interrupted.

'Well, of course there is, and you must sort it out, before she does something else desperate.' And Aunt Hazel began to cry, helpless, genuine tears running down her face.

Tarn found tissues, made tea and uttered comforting noises, but her brain was in free fall.

At least, she thought, a police investigation explained why visitors were being kept at bay. But what could Evie possibly have done to deserve it?

When the older woman was calmer, she said, 'Aunt Hazel, how did you find out—about the police, I mean.'

'Mrs Benson's nephew is a solicitor. You weren't doing anything to help, so he wrote a letter for me to that place, to insist on my being allowed to visit my poor little girl, and that's what he was told. He generally does wills and property, not police matters, so he didn't feel he could take it any further. But you must.'

Tarn said carefully, 'Aunt Hazel—was there anything going on in Evie's life that ever caused you concern—made you wonder?'

'Evie was always as good as gold.' Bright spots of colour appeared in Mrs Griffiths' cheeks. 'She had a wonderful life—until she met that dreadful Caspar Brandon creature who ruined it for her. I wish she'd never gone to work for his horrible company.'

'Do you know how long she was there—and what exactly her job was?'

'She was some kind of executive, and when she changed to that other place—the Scottish company—she was promoted to top management.'

'Scottish company?' Tarn echoed. 'What was that?'

'Oh, I can't remember. Mac something or other.' Mrs Griffiths hunted for another tissue. 'And why are you harping on about the past, when it's now that Evie needs help?'

But Tarn was suddenly remembering the paperwork she'd found at Evie's flat. She said, 'Was it the MacNaughton Company she went to?'

'It may have been.' Aunt Hazel sniffed. 'How can you expect me to think about trivia at a time like this?'

'I don't.' Tarn gave her a quick hug. 'And I give you my word I'll try and find out what's going on,' adding silently, *In all kinds of ways.*

The MacNaughton company occupied smart offices in Clerkenwell.

'Good afternoon.' Tarn smiled at the blonde receptionist. 'I was wondering if you could supply me with some information.'

The girl gave her a dubious look. 'If it's about a job, I should warn you that the company demands very high standards from our domestic and office cleaners, and requires at least three references.'

'It's nothing like that,' said Tarn. 'I wanted to

ask about a relation of mine who worked here quite recently, as some kind of executive.'

'I doubt that very much,' the other returned stonily. 'This is a family firm, owned and managed by Mr and Mrs MacNaughton, and their two sons.'

'But I'm sure I have the right company. My—cousin's name is Griffiths—Eve Griffiths.'

There was an odd silence, then the receptionist said, 'I can't help you, I'm afraid.'

'Is there someone else I could speak to—Mrs MacNaughton, perhaps.'

The girl shook her head. 'It's strict policy not to discuss past or present employees with anyone outside the firm. If you're related to Miss Griffiths, I suggest you ask her what you want to know. Good afternoon.' She opened a file on the desk in front of her and began checking figures with ostentatious care.

'Thank you,' Tarn said coldly. 'I will.'

But when I do, she thought as she left the building, will I find myself walking into yet another brick wall? Oh, Evie, what on earth have you been doing?

'I hear you've found a flat,' said Grace. She and Tarn were sitting in Fortnum and Mason's having tea. 'I'm amazed you could prise Caz out of his old one, but I suppose love will always find a way.'

Tarn smiled awkwardly. 'Oh, I don't think he minded too much.'

'Well, I wish we were having the same luck tracking down a wedding dress for you.' Grace poured the tea and proffered a plate of cream-filled pastries. She went on wistfully, 'Have you seen nothing at all you liked today?'

'I'm afraid not,' Tarn fibbed, adding more truthfully, 'But I feel really guilty dragging you all round London on a wild goose chase.'

'I'm glad of the exercise. I was beginning to vegetate quite seriously in our rural idyll.'

'Well, it seems to suit you. You look fabulous.'

'I look like a pumpkin on legs,' Grace retorted. 'I haven't bought a dress for your wedding either—just hired a small tent.' She paused. 'And while we're on the subject of appearance, if you'll forgive me for saying so, you're looking a little pale and heavy-eyed.' She gave a naughty giggle. 'Of course, there may be a very good reason for this, but you should be aiming for radiance on the big day.'

Tarn flushed. 'I think I'm probably suffering

from bridal nerves. Even for the tiniest wedding like ours there seems so much to do.'

Grace nodded. 'Tell me about it. I decided quite early on that I was in a no-win situation over the arrangements, so I stood back and let the respective mothers slug it out. It worked perfectly—for me anyway.'

She was silent for a moment, then said, 'Tarn—I know it's not really my business to be asking, but he's Brendan's best mate from way back, and I think the world of him too, so I'm going to say it anyway.' She drew a breath. 'You—you do love Caz, don't you?'

Tarn was reaching for her cup, and her hand jerked, spilling some tea in the saucer.

She achieved a breathless laugh. 'Yes—yes, of course I do. Why do you ask?'

Grace shrugged uncomfortably. 'I suppose—because it's all happened so fast.'

Tarn used a tissue to mop up the spilled tea. 'Also girl marries boss is a terrible cliché,' she said quietly.

'Well, knowing Caz's views on romance in the workplace, it has come as rather a surprise. Besides…' She stopped abruptly.

'Besides, you thought he was going to marry Ginny Fraser,' Tarn supplied.

Grace sighed. 'Let's say we were afraid it might happen. Which was one of many reasons why we were so delighted when he found you.' She smiled. 'Brendan always said it would happen like that. That Caz would meet someone and fall head over heels. And clearly he has.'

'But you're wondering if I've done the same.' Tarn stared down at the table. 'And as his friend, you're probably entitled to ask.' She drew a breath, then said, stumbling a little, 'I may not wear my heart on my sleeve, Grace, but I do love him, more than I ever dreamed possible, although I tried hard not to. And if I'm not turning cartwheels, it's because, frankly, I'm feeling stunned.'

She gestured helplessly. 'He's a millionaire several times over, for heaven's sake. And he takes so much about his life totally for granted—whereas I…'

'Fit into it just perfectly,' Grace said gently. 'But things haven't always been easy for him, Tarn. He's rich and good-looking and that can act like a magnet for some women.'

She frowned. 'For instance, he had a problem earlier this year with some idiotic female making a complete fool of herself over him.'

Tarn sent her a swift glance. 'Who was that?'

Grace shook her head. 'I don't know all the details, but Brendan says it was a real mess and took a lot of sorting.'

'Yes,' Tarn said bleakly. 'I'm sure it did.'

It was an effort to smile, but somehow she managed it. 'And now to prove my sincerity about my forthcoming nuptials, let's get a cab back to that place in Knightsbridge and take another look at that pretty cream silk. It's the only one that's really stayed in my mind, so maybe that's a good omen.'

They continued to laugh and chat all the way back to Knightsbridge and the purchase of a dress that she knew, as she paid for it, she would not be wearing on any occasion in her life.

Twenty-four hours. That was all the time she had left.

Tarn felt shaken and bewildered when she considered how quickly she had reached this point.

So many staging points along the way. So many games of 'let's pretend' with herself as the only participant.

The miles of furniture showrooms traversed.

The gallons of paint chosen for the team of decorators waiting to transform a flat she would never occupy.

The party at Brandon to wish Caz and herself

well and present them with a magnificent collection of crystal glassware.

Her ticket booked on a flight back to New York, in the first instance. And after that—who knew?

And now, the final act. The devastating, terrible letter that she had to write.

Closure.

Followed, presumably, by 'moving on'.

That comforting, meaningless phrase supposedly intended to salve the agony of a life torn up and thrown away, Tarn thought and shivered.

'I'm on my way.' Della emerged from her room with her travel bag slung over her shoulder.

She was taking two days of her holiday entitlement and spending them at her parents' home, because, as she said, she had no wish to be around when Caz Brandon came calling.

'That won't happen,' Tarn had told her, but Della had simply pursed her lips and said she preferred not to chance it.

Now, she gave Tarn a narrow-eyed look. 'Are you going to be all right?'

'Of course.' Tarn lifted her chin. 'After all, this is what I've been aiming for.'

'Have you booked a courier to deliver it?'

'Yes. It's all arranged.'

'And have you tipped off the Press, to make his

humiliation as public as it gets? Put the icing on the cake, just as you've always said?'

Tarn didn't look at her. 'Not yet,' she said. 'I—I'll write the letter first.'

'Well, don't forget,' Della cautioned. She gave Tarn a bracing hug. 'Be brave,' she whispered. 'You know you're doing the right thing.'

Am I? thought Tarn, when she was alone. With so many questions still unanswered, I'm not as sure. But I can't allow doubts to creep in. Not at this stage. I have to go on.

But an hour later and on her third draft, she was struggling. Her first attempt had sounded regretful; the second, apologetic. And that wasn't what she wanted at all.

I have to become Chameleon again, she thought. I have to detach myself and speak with someone else's voice. Tell it as if it was someone else's story.

Then maybe I can bear it.

'Caz,' she wrote eventually. 'There will be no marriage between us today or ever.

'I am leaving you, just as you abandoned Eve Griffiths, your former fiancée and my foster sister a few months ago.

'Eve, as you know, was so heartbroken and traumatised by your rejection of her that she tried to kill herself, and she is now a virtual prisoner in The Refuge, where you are a trustee.

'Presumably, you thought that once she was out of sight, she would also be out of mind. But not so.'

That was the right tone. Cool and dispassionate. Just relating the facts.

'Because Eve wrote me letter after letter, talking about you and your relationship with her. She believed her passionate love for you was returned, and was overjoyed at the prospect of becoming your wife. She was even naïve enough to think that the stones in the engagement ring you gave her were diamonds.

'She did not understand that you were simply stringing her along and had no intention of marrying her or that you would abandon her once you were tired of the brutal game you were playing with her heart and mind.

'As soon as she realised that, she tried to destroy herself, which was when I decided your cruelty and arrogance should be punished, and that you too should discover what it was like to be humiliated and deserted by someone you trusted. So I came to England to find you.

'No doubt you are used to thinking yourself irresistible to women, so you were, of course, ridiculously easy to fool.'

Oh, Caz—Caz...

'But now I'm the one tired of pretending, and it's time to bring the whole charade to an end.

'I hope you will have the decency to allow my foster sister to be released so that she can start to rebuild her life without further harassment from you or the police.

'Goodbye.'

She signed her name, folded the sheets of notepaper and put them in a padded envelope large enough to accommodate the box with his grandmother's ring as well.

But she couldn't bring herself to take it off quite yet. Knew how accustomed she had become to the glimmer of the stones and how bare her hand would seem without them.

'You're being sentimental,' she said aloud. 'And you can't afford that.' But the words were spoken without emotion or even conviction. And the ring stayed where it was.

In fact, she felt strangely blank, as if putting her accusations against him down on paper at last had somehow purged her of all the anger and bitterness that had brought her to this moment.

The evening stretched ahead of her like a wasteland, yet, at the same time, the walls of the flat seemed to be closing round her, leaving her feeling cramped and uneasy. No matter where she looked in the room, the envelope seemed to be in her sight lines, waiting.

And there was something else that must go into it before it was sealed, she reminded herself. The key to the new flat.

She remembered their first viewing of it, the whole top floor of an apartment building from an earlier century with high ceilings and large windows. How she'd walked from room to room at his side, in spite of herself almost breathless with excitement. Imagining the flat neutral colours on the walls replaced by something with more depth and glow—a gleaming ivory in the sitting room perhaps as a backdrop for Caz's pictures.

Space and light, she thought. And, in the master bedroom's en suite, a shower big enough for two.

'I hardly dare ask,' Caz had said softly when the agent had withdrawn tactfully into another room. 'But do you feel about it as I do? Do you think we could make it into a home?'

For a moment, she was silent, recognising the enormity of what was happening. When she spoke, it was in a voice she hardly recognised, expressing a truth she could not avoid or dissemble.

She'd said simply, 'I could be happy here.'

And knew that her words concealed a world of regret.

She hadn't been there for several days, so she had no idea how it looked now that their decorating ideas had been put into operation.

'You've got to promise me you won't go and peek,' Caz had said, laughing. 'I want it to be a surprise.'

But I mustn't think about that, she told herself. Not any more, or I shall go crazy. And switched on the television, looking for distraction.

'Starting next,' a disembodied voice informed her, 'is a new series, The Body Politic, which will take a close look at parliamentary democracy in the whole of the United Kingdom. The presenter is Ginny Fraser.'

'Some distraction,' Tarn muttered, her throat tightening painfully as she reached for the remote control. 'And the last person I want to see.'

Caz would probably go back to Ginny in the end, she thought, finding consolation in taking up where he'd left off. Her mouth twisted as she visualised Grace's reaction.

Then she stilled. Brendan and Grace, she thought, imagining their shock and anger when she failed to show. What would Caz say to them?

What explanation could he possibly offer? Or would it come as no surprise because they'd known about Evie and her part in his life all along?

She found she did not want to believe that.

Do something useful, she told herself as she got up restlessly and fetched her bag. The key to the new flat was in an inside pocket, and she held it in the palm of her hand, looking down at it. Struggling with herself as temptation beckoned.

Where would be the harm, she thought, in taking one last look? Caz's ban had not been serious. Besides, he would never know, she assured herself. It was the eve of his wedding, so he would be enjoying his stag night, celebrating what he supposed would be his last night of freedom.

And, anyway, she needed to say goodbye.

She slipped a thin jacket over her dress and went out to find a cab.

Even as she was paying off the driver, she was still hesitant, but at the same time knew there was little point in turning round and going meekly back to the empty silence she'd left.

She tapped in the entry code at the front door, and rode up in the lift to the top floor.

'There's a roof garden here too.' She could hear

Caz's voice. 'But the tubs are filled with flowers, not hot water.'

She unlocked the door and stepped into the hall, pausing for a moment to inhale the clean smell of paint and newly varnished wood floors.

She went first to the sitting room, halting with an involuntary cry of pleasure. The furniture that they'd been told would take several weeks to arrive had been delivered and unpacked. Only Caz's pictures, placed carefully in a corner, were still in their wrappings.

The image in her head had become reality and it was beautiful, she thought, swallowing.

She turned away, her eyes blurring suddenly. She was heading for the kitchen but on an impulse opened the door to the master bedroom instead.

Someone had been busy here too, she saw as she walked slowly forward, because the bed had been made up with the creamy linen they'd chosen, and the exquisite coverlet, like a golden sunburst, was folded neatly across its foot.

I could be happy here...

She closed her eyes and stood, motionless, her arms clasped around her body, until the sudden, tingling moment when she realised she was no longer alone.

She turned slowly and looked at Caz, leaning in the doorway.

He said, 'So you couldn't keep away.'

'Nor could you.' She was trembling inside, the blood singing in her veins. She spoke huskily. 'I—I thought you'd be out on the town with friends.'

'Getting blasted?' His own tone was faintly caustic. 'Not very flattering to one's bride, I've always thought. Anyway, I went out a few nights ago for a quiet dinner with Brendan and a few other friends.'

'Oh,' she said. 'I see.' She paused. There was tension in the room, warm and living like an electric current. She touched the tip of her tongue to her dry mouth, searching for something to say. 'They haven't hung the pictures in the sitting room.'

'No,' he said. 'I thought we'd do that together, when we came back from our honeymoon.'

'Yes,' she said. 'That's a—lovely idea.'

How can you look at me? she wanted to scream. How can you be so blind as not to see what I mean to do to you?

Aloud, she said, 'It all looks wonderful. Better than I ever dreamed.' She shook her head. 'But I'm sorry if I've ruined your surprise.'

He said slowly, 'You haven't spoiled a thing.'

She went on quickly, 'You see—I just needed so very much to see it.'

Caz moved away from the doorway and walked forward, halting a few yards away, the hazel eyes tender and hungry as he looked at her.

'How strange you should feel like that,' he said. 'Because, although I didn't know it, I also needed—so very much—to see you here.'

He held out his arms and Tarn ran to him like a homing bird, a sob rising in her throat.

Their mouths met and clung with a stark and heated urgency.

And when he lifted her and carried her to the bed, Tarn knew she could no longer deny him. Or herself.

CHAPTER TWELVE

THE mattress felt soft and yielding as Caz placed her gently down upon it. She stared up at him, aware of the thunder of her heart, and the soft trembling building inside her that she knew, in spite of her comparative inexperience, was born of excitement, not fear.

Yet as he turned to switch on the ivory-shaded lamp on the night table, she sat up, reaching for his arm. 'No—please.'

'Ah, but I need to see you, darling,' he told her huskily. 'I want you to look at me too. So—no darkness between us. Not tonight, Tarn, my love. Not ever.'

She watched as he began to strip, his movements totally un-self-conscious, until he wore only his shorts, the cling of the silk in no way concealing the stark reality of his arousal. And when he came at last to lie beside her, drawing her close, she went to him without reserve.

They lay, wrapped in each other's arms, bathed

in the soft light falling across the bed, exchanging slow, sweet kisses. And when, at last, he looked at her, a question in his gaze, she lifted a hand and touched his cheek, sliding her finger along the firm line of his mouth. He captured its tip with his lips, suckling it gently, making her feel the heat building inside her, and the sudden frantic scald of desire between her thighs as she wound her arms around his neck, lifting herself towards him in mute offering.

He began to undress her, his hands moving without haste, but with heart-stopping purpose as he dealt with the fastenings on her clothes and laid them aside, one by one.

When her last covering had gone, he stared down at her, his eyes rapt, almost wondering.

He said shakily, 'Oh, God, you're so lovely. More beautiful than I could have dreamed. I'm almost scared to touch you. Scared I'll lose control and ruin everything for you.'

'You won't,' she whispered. She took his hand and carried it in promise and reassurance to her breast, gasping as his fingers cupped the soft, scented mound. As he stroked her nipple with the ball of his thumb, arousing it to swift aching life. As his mouth took hers once more with deep and passionate urgency, parting her lips with his to allow the hot searching invasion of his tongue.

She touched him in her turn, running her hands along the hard muscularity of his shoulders, letting her fingers drift questingly down the long, lithe spine until she reached the band of his shorts and slid her hands under the silk to find his firm, flat buttocks, instinct guiding her in how to mould and caress them.

Caz uttered a sound between a laugh and groan, the breath catching in his throat as at last he moved, discarding the shorts completely, then lifted Tarn, placing her against the heaped pillows, bending his head to kiss her breasts, his tongue laving their tautly sensitive peaks in an exquisite and irresistible torment that forced a startled moan from her lips.

She could feel the hardness of him pressing against her and she reached down clasping the rigid, velvety shaft, shyly at first, then with growing confidence, as she ran her fingers along its proud length, cupping and caressing him, and felt his whole body shudder with pleasure in response.

His hands were exploring her too in intimate detail, spanning her waist, skimming the slender curves of her hips, smoothing the concavity of her belly, every stroke of his fingers on her skin a potent and erotic delight, taking him nearer and nearer to the soft, downy junction of her parted thighs.

Tarn's head moved restlessly on the pillow as she tried and failed to control an involuntary sob of yearning. An open and unmistakable sign of how much she wanted the total consummation of their mutual desire. How she longed to belong to him completely at last.

And heard him whisper, 'Wait, my sweet. Wait just a little.'

But it seemed an eternity before he touched her *there* at the sweet, melting, molten core of her. Before she felt the subtle glide of his fingertips penetrating the soft satin folds of her womanhood in lingering, unhurried incitement.

Tarn felt the startled flurry of her breathing as one by one she found herself surrendering all the barriers to her deepest senses that she'd carefully constructed in response to this new and powerful intimacy, her body boneless, her eyes shadowed as she stared up into the dark, intent and tender face above her.

As she felt his smile touch her lips and welcomed again the enticing flicker of his tongue against hers.

His hand moved, claiming her tiny hidden peak,

stroking it deftly but so very gently that at first she was hardly conscious of what he was doing to her until she realised that his soft, rhythmic caress was creating a whole new world of delicate almost fugitive sensations.

Her bewildered mind and body sought them, held them captive, her concentration focussing almost blindly now on the exquisite play of his fingers, their pressure increasing now, circling on her with sensuous purpose, inviting her to experience a pleasure she had never known before, nor even imagined could exist.

Every inch of her skin seemed to be quivering, the blood pulsing almost audibly in her veins, her entire being enslaved by this new and devastating intensity.

She was like a leaf caught in a tide, carried inexorably towards some brink under the irresistible urging of his hands and mouth.

His name was a husky moan forced from her throat, and then, in the next second, she was lost, her last vestiges of control shattered, as she was lifted up by a mounting spiral of shivering, sobbing delight until her body convulsed into its first spasms of sheer rapture.

She cried out again into the heat of his mouth,

her voice cracked and incoherent, her hands biting into his shoulders.

And in that moment felt him slide his hands under her hips and enter her, sheathing himself in the pulsating inner sweetness that he had so gently but so surely created.

Briefly, he was still, then he began to move, as if emphasising his possession, thrusting into her slowly and deeply, filling her again and again with his strength and power.

Gasping, Tarn lifted her legs, locking them round him, letting her own body echo the rhythm he had initiated, giving herself without restraint, taking him into her with utter acceptance—utter completeness. Absorbing—glorying in the total difference of this sensation to everything that had gone before.

Finding herself at last a woman in union with her man.

And when the pace of their joining quickened, she made his urgency her own, answering the fierce drive of his loins with her own passion. Hearing him call out to her, his voice almost agonised, as he came.

Afterwards, she held him, pillowing his head on her breasts and feeling the dampness of tears on her face.

He knew at once.

'Darling—I hurt you...'

'No,' she whispered. 'Don't you see? I—I'm crying because I'm happy. That's all.'

Caz was silent for a moment then he said huskily, 'That's everything. My dearest love.'

Tarn awoke to early daylight and silence. She stretched slowly, eyes still shut, her bewildered mind acknowledging that her body was glowing with a sense of acute well-being that she had never experienced before, or believed could exist.

And with that, memories—images—of the previous night and just how often they'd turned to each other in mutual, laughing joy, came swarming into her consciousness, and she understood exactly why she felt as she did, her lips parting on a startled sound between a gasp and a laugh, as she reached across the bed to find the creator of this miracle.

But there was no warm man sleeping there, and the space beside her was chilly as if it had been empty for some time. She sat up sharply, the sheet falling away from her naked body, as she stared around her, alert for the sound of movement elsewhere in the flat, yet hearing nothing.

It was then she saw the folded sheet of paper on

the adjoining pillow, and opened it with fingers that shook slightly, to read the few lines he'd left for her.

'My darling,' he'd written. 'I was watching you sleep when I suddenly remembered it's supposed to be unlucky for the bride and groom to meet on their wedding day before the ceremony. I reckon we've blown that particular superstition to kingdom come, but have decided to avoid further risks.

'So, my sweet, I'll see you again very soon at the register office, although I have to tell you that nothing can make you any more my wife than you are at this moment.'

He'd signed it simply, 'Caz.'

Tarn read it again, then dropped it as if the paper had scorched her fingers.

She should be thankful, she thought, her breathing quickening, that he had decided to leave without waking her, or she might not have been able to let him go at all. She could well have clung to him, forgetting everything but the need to be with him. To stay with him, and be his woman, his wife for all eternity.

Instead, she'd been spared to do what she must. To finish what she'd started. And the time had now come.

For a moment the room blurred, but she fought

back the tears. There was no place for them now. They must wait.

Twenty minutes later, washed and dressed, she was heading off. She'd fully intended to leave his note behind, but at the last moment, just as she reached the front door, something impelled her to go back to the bedroom and retrieve it.

'And how many kinds of fool does that make me?' she wondered unhappily as she pushed it into her bag.

The hotel she'd picked near the airport was big, busy and anonymous, all points in its favour. She checked in, arranged to hire a car for her visit to The Refuge the following morning, then went up to her room, where she remained, at intervals trying to read, or trying to doze or trying to watch television, but accomplishing none of these aims.

She ordered a meal from room service, and ate half of it. She opened some wine from the mini bar and drank none of it. She walked up and down the room, her arms wrapped round her body, trying not to think what would have happened earlier in the day at the register office, but unable to rid her mind of it.

At first, he'd probably thought she was held up in traffic, or exercising a bride's prerogative to be late. But then, as the minutes passed, he must have begun to wonder, until, of course, the arrival of the courier with her letter made everything more than clear.

But at least she hadn't notified the Press. In the end, she had spared him because she couldn't bring herself to twist the knife by making the necessary calls. So, in effect, no-one would know of his humiliation except Brendan and Grace, who would naturally say nothing.

And by the time the news got to the London office, Caz would no doubt have found some excuse for his continued bachelordom. He could say they'd discovered they weren't suited after all. Even that it had been a lucky escape on both sides.

Or he might employ the same reasoning that he'd used with Evie, she thought, trying to fire up her anger and sense of self-justification.

Not easy, when all she wanted to do was cry until she had no tears left. But that couldn't be allowed yet.

Who ever said revenge was sweet? she asked herself, as pain lanced her. Because they were wrong. It was savage and bitter, and no-one could remain immune from its effects. Least of all, the person who had set the whole thing in motion.

I could have said 'Not my problem' and stayed

in New York, she thought. But I promised Uncle Frank I'd watch out for the two of them. And fight their battles if necessary.

And I have to believe that this was a just war. I must. Because I have no choice.

So, tomorrow morning, I shall go to Evie and tell her that she's avenged. That Caz Brandon now knows in his heart and soul the damage he's inflicted, and is paying for it.

And that she has nothing further to fear from him, and can start on the road to complete recovery.

Whereas I—I have another road to tread, and I can see nothing ahead of me but desolation. And no way back. Starting with tonight…

'She's much better this morning,' Nurse Farlow informed her briskly as she led the way up to Evie's room. 'Quite chipper, in fact. Mind you, the police haven't been back this week, which helps.'

'I don't quite understand.' Tarn spoke carefully. Her head was aching and her eyes felt as if they had been scoured with grit. She had spent most of the night staring into the darkness, too emotionally exhausted to sleep, or attempt to make positive plans. But now there were things she needed to know. 'Why did they want to interview her in the first place?'

She received a faintly caustic look. 'That's something you need to ask her yourself—if she'll tell you. But don't count on it.'

The older woman paused. 'I gather we won't be seeing you again. That you're leaving England.'

'I never intended to stay,' Tarn said. 'I only came over for Evie's sake. And if she's on the mend, hopefully her mother can start visiting in my place.'

The response was a dubious shrug, and a muttered 'Perhaps.'

Not nearly as hopeful as I thought, Tarn told herself ruefully as they walked along Evie's landing. The door of her room was open, and a cleaning trolley was standing outside.

Tarn was mentally bracing herself for the coming interview when the air was suddenly split by a shrill, wailing scream, then the word, 'No!' shouted over and over again.

The nurse pushed past Tarn, throwing 'Wait.' over her shoulder.

But there was no way Tarn was going to stand meekly in the corridor when Evie was in trouble, and she rushed into the room on Nurse Farlow's heels.

Evie was crouched in her chair, shaking, hands over her face, making strangled guttural sounds. Beside her, a white-faced woman in a crisp overall was trying ineffectually to calm her by patting her shoulder.

'What's going on here?' Nurse Farlow demanded.

The cleaner shook her head, looking terrified. 'I don't know, nurse, I'm sure. I had my Daily Gazette on the trolley, and she asked if she could see it. I didn't see any harm so I gave it to her. Then all this started.'

The paper in question was lying scattered on the floor, as if it had been thrown there.

Tarn bent, gathering the sheets together. As she straightened, she found herself staring down at the front page. At a picture of a man walking down some steps from a building, his head bent. At the headline above it, proclaiming 'Billionaire's Wedding Shock'. And at the text beneath it.

'Publishing tycoon Caspar Brandon wanted a quiet wedding,' she read in horror. 'But what he got was total silence when his mystery bride, former employee Tarn Desmond, failed to show up yesterday for the ceremony at Blackwell Registry Office.

'Brandon (34) who has escorted a series of beautiful women in the past, including TV Personality of the Year Ginny Fraser, raised eyebrows at a recent company gala when he announced his engagement to the unknown Miss Desmond who worked as a junior editor on one of his magazines.

'As he left the registry office alone, the jilted groom refused to speak to reporters. And a representative from Brandon International issued a firm "No comment."

'Efforts to trace Miss Desmond have so far failed.'

But this can't have happened, Tarn told herself, feeling cold and sick. Because I didn't tell them. I didn't...

And only realised she'd spoken the words aloud when there was another hysterical screech from Evie.

'You've dared to come here, you bitch.' She was glaring at Tarn as if she loathed her, spittle on her lips. 'You of all people? You were supposed to be on my side, but all this time you've really been trying to take my Caz away from me. Marry him yourself.'

Tarn stared at her. 'But Evie—you know that isn't true...'

'I know that it's me he really wants, and it always will be.' The younger girl's face was ugly, mottled with rage, her eyes blazing. 'Now get out of here. Out of our lives.' Her voice rose. 'You'll never have him, because I won't let you.'

The quivering heap in the chair was suddenly transformed, launching herself at Tarn with the speed of a striking snake. Taken unawares, Tarn was knocked to the floor by the sheer force of the attack, and cried out in pain as Evie's nails raked down her face.

The room was suddenly filled with people, the Professor himself pulling Evie away, holding her firmly, her arms behind her back, while he spoke to her quietly and gently.

Tarn scrambled to her knees and then, awkwardly, to her feet, unable to believe what had just happened.

She said unevenly, 'Evie, I don't understand. What is all this? I was only doing what you wanted. What we agreed. You know that.'

The Professor glanced round at her, his expression impatient. 'Doctor Rahendra, will you please see to this young woman's face, then take her to my office? And I'd be obliged if you'd also ask my secretary to organise some coffee.'

A slim pretty girl in a white coat, with olive skin and a thick plait of glossy dark hair, came to Tarn and took her arm. 'If you will come with me.'

'No, not yet.' Tarn tried to tug herself free. 'I want to know what's going on.'

'The Professor will speak to you presently. Explain everything.' Doctor Rahendra's voice was kind but firm. 'But now you must leave here. Our patient finds your presence disturbing. And those scratches are deep. They need attention.'

In a spotless treatment room, Tarn winced as her cheek was bathed with antiseptic, and cream applied.

'They are a little unsightly, but they will heal more quickly without a dressing,' the doctor told her. She added. 'And you will not be scarred.'

Tarn bent her head. 'Am I supposed to find that a comfort?' she asked dully. 'There are worse things than scars.'

The other nodded. 'The reaction of Miss Griffiths has shocked you deeply. That is quite natural.' She sighed. 'And it is all the more unfortunate when we believed she was making progress at last. But clearly we were being too optimistic as the Professor has warned us all along.'

She walked to the door. 'Now I will take you to him.'

The Professor was standing looking out of the window when Tarn was shown into his room.

He turned and gave her a frowning glance. 'I

permitted this visit in order for you to say good-bye, Miss Griffiths—or should I now call you Miss Desmond. I did not intend it to provoke another crisis.'

Tarn lifted her chin. 'Nor did I. In fact, I thought my sister would welcome the news that our plan had succeeded.'

'And what plan was that precisely?' He came back to his desk and sat down, reaching for the coffee pot standing on a tray in front of him, and filling two cups.

'As you know, Evie was having a relationship with a very rich, very attractive man.' Tarn kept her tone impersonal, as she accepted her cup. Sipped the strong brew. 'She was actually planning her wedding when he suddenly terminated their engagement. I—I understood it was the trauma of that break-up that triggered her suicide attempt.'

She took a steadying breath. 'He'd treated her abominably and I decided he should undergo the same fate. Suffer the same humiliation.'

He nodded. 'Acting for the benefit of female humanity, I suppose.'

Tarn said hotly, 'You find this amusing?'

'No,' he returned. 'Tragic. And with a little

frankness, it could have been stopped at the out-set. And for that, I must blame myself.'

'It's gracious of you to admit it.'

'Oh, it's not on your behalf, Miss Desmond. If I'd spoken, I might have saved one of our re-spected trustees, Caspar Brandon from trial by tabloid, among other things.' He shook his head. 'All along some instinct told me I shouldn't trust you, but that was for a rather different reason.'

'How dare you criticise me.' Her voice shook. 'Everything I've done has been in good faith—and because Evie herself begged me to help her. I wasn't acting alone. She wanted him punished. Needed him to feel some of the agony he'd caused her, and I agreed because I—I thought that would help her recover.'

'And what cod psychology books have you been reading, Miss Desmond?'

'I don't need to read anything to know that she's terrified of your so-called "respected trustee",' Tarn retorted. 'I don't know what threats he's made to keep her quiet about their affair—apart from locking her in here for the duration, but they've certainly worked.'

She drew a breath. 'And if what happened just now is a result of your treatment, heaven help the rest of the poor souls being kept here.'

'Amen to that,' he said unexpectedly. 'Sometimes, I wish I could call on divine intervention. Usually I have to rely on common sense. Which I signally failed to use in this particular case.'

He gave a brief harsh sigh. 'But that stops now, because there are a few things you need to know about your foster sister. Firstly, she is not in this institution simply because she miscalculated the number of illegal pills involved in her supposed suicide attempt. She had already agreed to accept out-patient treatment here as an alternative to serious legal proceedings against her.'

Tarn was suddenly rigid. 'On what possible grounds?'

'There is a choice.' He ticked them off on his fingers. 'Theft, drug dealing, wilful damage, assault and, of course, stalking. There was talk of a restraining order among other measures.'

The words were like blows, thudding against her ribs, making it difficult to breathe. She said hoarsely, 'I don't believe you. Evie wouldn't do those things. She couldn't...'

'She could, Miss Desmond, and she did. You've been working abroad, I believe, so you've been out of close touch with your family for quite a while.' He paused. 'But you were clearly doing well, and that, we feel, was part of the problem. Eve also wanted your earning power and what went with it. But as you know, she had no real qualifications and found it hard to find work that paid decent money or indeed hold down a job at all.

'However, she eventually managed to obtain employment with a highly reputable cleaning firm.'

Tarn said faintly, 'The MacNaughton Company?'

He nodded. 'The very same. At first she worked in their office cleaning section, where her performance appeared satisfactory, then, at her own request, she transferred to the domestic field, where she worked for some very wealthy clients, not all of whom, I fear, were as careful with their possessions as they should have been. And as your sister was permanently short of money, she succumbed to temptation, and began to steal from some of them.'

He frowned. 'There was no actual proof, of course, but a couple of them took their suspicions to MacNaughton and Evelyn was dismissed.'

'But she was living at home,' Tarn protested. 'She couldn't have been that badly paid.'

'She wasn't,' said the Professor. 'But by this time, she'd moved into a flat she could not afford, so she needed an alternative source of income.

And eventually, because of her MacNaughton connections, she found one.'

She stared at him. 'But I don't understand any of this. Surely Caz—Mr Brandon—was paying for the flat.'

He said with a trace of impatience, 'My dear Miss Desmond, I doubt whether at that point he was even aware of her existence, although that was soon to change,' he added grimly.

'Not—aware?' There was a hollow feeling in the pit of Tarn's stomach. 'I don't understand. He—they were lovers. Engaged to be married. You must know that.'

'No,' the Professor said more gently. 'I'm afraid all that was pure imagination on her part. She saw him while she was working at Brandon, fell for him and created a fantasy in her own mind, which she built up when she began cleaning his apartment until it reached danger levels, and beyond.'

He shook his head. 'Evelyn has never had a relationship with Caz Brandon, Miss Desmond. She has been lying from the start to everyone—most damagingly to herself.'

He paused, then added heavily, 'But also, it seems, lying particularly to you. Her hated rival.'

CHAPTER THIRTEEN

TARN felt numb and deathly cold, as if she was seeing the Professor through a wall of ice. His words seemed to sting at her brain.

She said, stumbling a little, 'You're saying she hates me? But why? She only found out about what I've done to Caz just now, so it can't be that.' She swallowed. 'Surely it's not because I went to America—and have a career? She's jealous of *that*?'

'That's only part of it,' the Professor said quietly. 'She has always felt you were her father's favourite, and resented it. Both she and her mother apparently looked on you as an outsider—a cuckoo in the nest.'

Tarn bent her head. 'I think I always knew that. But he—Uncle Frank—was so good to me, and I knew he wanted me to make sure they were all right. So I tried to do that for his sake.' She spread her hands helplessly. 'Yet Evie wrote me all those letters detailing her affair with Caz. Why did she do that?'

'It was all part of the illusion. She needed to prove she could outdo you in one area at least. To make you jealous as well.'

'You mean—this whole horrible thing is my fault?' Her voice broke.

'Certainly not.' His tone was brisk. 'Your mistake lay in believing your foster sister was still the child you'd grown up with, and were fond of, and you can't be blamed for that.' He paused. 'Even though you've undoubtedly been culpable in other ways.'

Tarn thought of the newspaper photograph, with Caz's face drawn and haggard, and winced at the pain which tore through her.

She said in a low voice, 'And for that I'm being well and truly punished, please believe that.'

She paused, taking a deep steadying breath, because there was so much more she needed to know. 'What exactly did Evie do? To Caz, I mean?'

'Went through the things in his flat. Took some shirts, some underwear, a pair of shoes to keep at her own place, to bolster her fantasy that they were in a relationship.' He sounded almost matter of fact. 'Removed and probably destroyed photographs that appeared to relate to other women. Read his desk diary then followed him to social engagements, blagging her way in.'

Tarn tensed, feeling a swift wave of nausea as she remembered how she had first forced herself on his attention. 'Oh, God, that's so awful.'

'It gets worse.' The Professor pursed his lips. 'While she was working for MacNaughton, she'd had the keys to his apartment copied. When she was still unable to gain his attention in the way she wanted, she tried to hack into his computer, and when that failed, she took a hammer to it. Wrote messages in lipstick on his mirrors. Slashed a valuable painting.

'Eventually she began approaching him in public and making scenes, until finally, in a restaurant, she threw a glass of wine over his companion, who was not, and I quote, the dirty bitch he was screwing—but a visiting editor from Canada.'

He frowned. 'By that time the police were involved, of course.'

She bit her lip. 'I—I suppose he had no choice.'

'Oh, Mr Brandon didn't begin it.' His voice was reassuring. 'Miss Griffiths was already under investigation over the supply of illegal drugs. The husband of one of her former MacNaughton clients had become concerned about his wife's odd mood swings and found some pills hidden in a drawer.

'He showed them to his brother, a doctor who raised the alarm, and the wife confessed that she'd been obtaining private supplies of this particular tranquilliser from her former cleaner. At extortionate expense, naturally.'

Tarn shook her head. 'This is unbelievable,' she said, half to herself. 'How on earth could Evie—*Evie*—possibly have got hold of such things?'

'She'd been targeted by a dealer, of course,' said the Professor. 'While she was still working for MacNaughton and had access to bored, rich women who found their doctors unsympathetic to their problems. The ideal set-up from his point of view.' He paused. 'And from hers, especially as by this time her financial problems were pressing. In order to gain access to the kind of places Mr Brandon frequented, she needed an entirely new image—a wardrobe she couldn't afford.'

He shook his head. 'In such places, she was naturally able to find new contacts needing sleeping tablets, diet pills and tranquillisers. People who didn't ask questions or worry about the cost. Being young and pretty, she built up a remunerative business, but unfortunately she got greedy, and imposed a private surcharge of her own.

'However, when her supplier found out, things became—difficult for her.' He added flatly, 'Mr Brandon had offered to drop the stalking and malicious damage charges against her if she agreed to have therapy, but she was desperate for somewhere to hide, and this seemed the ideal sanctuary. So she deliberately staged the suicide attempt, knowing she'd be offered immediate residential care, but misjudged the dose.'

He smiled grimly. 'You assumed when she spoke of being frightened that she was referring to Mr Brandon, but you were wrong.'

'But her diary,' Tarn said desperately. 'She talked about him there too. You must have read that for yourself.'

'Ah,' he said. 'The references to "C", which you interpreted as Caz, but which was actually her former partner in crime. A man who lived in the flat above hers called Clayton. Roy Clayton.'

Tarn stared at him in horror. 'My God, I met him once, when I cleared out her things.'

'Then perhaps you can understand why she was scared,' he said drily. 'A thoroughly nasty piece of work. He even managed to get a message to her in here reminding her that she owed him money, and warning her to keep her mouth shut.'

Tarn gasped. 'But how could that happen? Security's so tight.'

'Unfortunately through a member of the kitchen staff, who believed quite sincerely she was passing on a love letter from a boyfriend, and has since been dismissed.'

Tarn got out of her chair and went to the window, pushing it open and gulping deep breaths of sunlit air. Behind her the phone rang, and she heard the Professor murmur a few quiet words before replacing the receiver.

When she could speak, she said, 'I'm sorry. I know that I'm keeping you from your work. But, you see, I keep telling myself that none of this is true. That it's just a nightmare and I'll wake up soon. Please tell me I'm right.'

'I'm afraid I can't do that, Miss Desmond. It's all too real.'

'I suppose so.' She turned slowly. 'And Evie—what will happen to her now—and in the future?'

'A lot will depend on the assistance she gives to the police investigation over the drugs racket. But I shall do my utmost to ensure she remains here. As Mr Brandon so quickly and generously recognised, she needs help rather than punishment.'

He gave a sharp sigh. 'Unfortunately, she is still using her delusions about him as a shield and an excuse for the rest of her behaviour. I am only sorry that you believed her and were drawn in.'

Tarn forced a smile. 'She—seemed to need me. That was my delusion. Perhaps it always has been.'

'But at least you won't be fighting against your return to reality, Miss Desmond, so your recovery should be swift and complete. And you'll find your own life is waiting for you.'

Tarn turned back to the window, her throat tightening. 'I'm afraid your prognosis is wrong, Professor. I was stupid and gullible, and because of that I've deliberately wrecked my life and thrown away the only chance of real happiness that will ever come to me.

'All I have left now is my career, and, believe me, that's no comfort.'

Her voice choked into a sudden uncontrollable sob and the sunlight blurred as the floodgates opened and she began to cry at last, tears pouring helplessly down her face, scalding her skin and burning in her throat.

A box of tissues was placed silently beside her on the window ledge, and a moment later the sound of the door closing told her the Professor had left the room.

She was thankful for it. She didn't require sympathy, counselling or criticism. She needed only to be alone to mourn the self-imposed destruction of her life. To face up to the fact that she'd been a fool and worse than a fool to take Evie's story at face value, or to think her concern and affection for her foster family had ever been reciprocated, at least by the female members.

And above all, she wanted to rage inwardly with grief and despair over the eternal emptiness ahead of her. Knowing—accepting that she had no-one to blame but herself, and would have to live with that for the remainder of her life.

Realising that Caz would never again take her in his arms. That she would have to forget the seductive warmth of his mouth, and the murmur of his voice as they made love. That she could not turn in the night and find him beside her.

That she would be—completely alone.

She yielded herself up to the storm of her misery, head bent, hands braced against the wall, her whole body shaking, gasping and choking, hearing herself making harsh, painful noises in her throat like a small wounded animal as the weeping tore her apart.

For an endless time, it seemed at the beginning as if she might never be able to stop, but, very gradually, the first desperate agonies of her remorse began to subside, leaving an aching emptiness in their place.

When at last she straightened, she had managed to establish a modicum of self-command, enough, anyway, to take a handful of tissues and began to blot her eyes and remove the worst ravages of grief from her face.

Not much, she thought, an occasional sob still catching her breath, but it was a start. A first step in a long, weary journey.

As she heard the door behind her re-open, she deliberately braced herself, her fingers grasping the window ledge as she took a deep, steadying breath.

'I'm sorry to have turned you out of your office, Professor Wainwright.' Trying to sound positive was difficult enough, but attempting to disguise the huskiness of her voice was quite impossible. 'I—I really didn't mean to lose control like that, but I seem to have been crying inside for so long now that I suppose it was almost bound to happen. You see I—I never thought it was possible to hurt so much.'

She paused. 'I know you must want to be rid of

me, but before I go, may I ask for one last favour. You'll be seeing Mr Brandon at some point, in his role as trustee, and perhaps you could find a moment in private to tell him that I'm sorry—for everything. And that I don't expect him to forgive me, because I'll never be able to forgive myself.'

She hesitated again. 'There's so much else I want to say, but it's probably best to leave it at that. So, will you—could you do that, please? I'd be eternally grateful.'

'Professor Wainwright has been detained,' Caz said quietly. 'So perhaps it would be more convenient if you gave the rest of your message to me in person.'

The room seemed to shiver and tilt, but somehow Tarn kept on her feet. A voice in her head was frantically whispering, 'No, oh, God, please no. I'm not ready for this. I can't bear it.'

Only now there were no more choices to be had, and she knew it, so she turned slowly and faced him across the room, her heart thudding against her ribcage like a trip hammer.

He was wearing denim pants and a dark blue shirt, open at the neck, and with the sleeves rolled up. He looked unutterably weary, the lines of his face deeply incised and he needed a shave.

She fought the tenderness rising within her, and

the yearning to go to him, taking his face between her hands, and kissing the grim tautness of his mouth. Because as she'd been telling herself over and over again, it was all a million years too late, and there was nothing to be done but stand her ground and endure his justified anger and whatever penance he might exact.

She said, 'What are you doing here?'

'It seemed the obvious place to find you. I knew that you'd be paying a last visit to your sister to tell her how well your plan had succeeded before you finally vanished back where you came from, and Jack Wainwright confirmed it for me.' His tone was flat. 'But I also knew that it wouldn't work out as you expected, and now you know it too. Don't you?'

'Yes.' She was glad she had no more tears to shed because weeping in front of him might be construed as a plea for mercy, and there could be none. They were standing on opposite sides of some great abyss and she couldn't reach him.

He looked at her more closely, his eyes narrowing, his brows drawing into a frown. 'What's happened to your face?'

'I already told you. When I heard the truth about Evie, I—lost it for a while. Didn't your friend the

Professor tell you he'd left me to get over my cry-ing jag?'

'No, he came down because he had other things he needed to say to me. And I was referring to the marks on your face, not the fact you look half-drowned.'

She lifted a defensive hand to her cheek. 'Evie went for me when she saw the newspaper story. It isn't serious.'

'Ah,' he said. 'I think that might depend on one's point of view.'

Tarn moved swiftly, restively. 'Caz—I don't know how the Press found out about the wed-ding, but I swear I didn't tell them. I—was going to, but I changed my mind. Someone else must have done it.'

'Your missing flatmate perhaps?'

She bit her lip. 'I—suppose so. I think she re-alised I wouldn't go through with it. She'd never agreed with what I was doing before, and had ar-gued with me about it, until she saw Evie's sup-posed engagement ring. She knew of course that they weren't real diamonds, and then she got angry too, and thought you deserved everything you got.'

'Of course she did,' he said. 'I'd never realised

before how compelling circumstantial evidence could be.'

'Nor had I,' she said. 'Although I'm not offering that as an excuse for what I've done.' She drew a deep breath. 'Caz, I don't know why you followed me here, but please believe that there's nothing you can say to me that will make me feel any worse about what's happened. So won't you accept that I'll never forgive myself for what I've done to you and just—let me go?'

He said quite gently, 'No, Tarn. I'm afraid I can't do that.'

There was a bleak hollow inside her. She said, 'I suppose it was too much to hope for. And I can't really blame you for wanting retribution.'

'If I did,' Caz said slowly, 'one look at you would change my mind. You're hardly a glowing advertisement for the benefits of revenge, my sweet.'

She said hoarsely, 'You're laughing at me?'

'Christ, no.' His tone sharpened. 'I've never been further from amusement in my life. And, yes, I was angry and hurt and humiliated, and all the other miserable fates you wished on me for the sake of that pathetic girl upstairs. And if you'd asked me there and then if I ever wanted to see you again, I'd have answered in the negative with no expletives deleted.

'But spending last night wide awake and alone, I came to a number of very different conclusions. For one thing, I realised you could have no idea what Eve Griffiths was and what she'd done. You simply believed the tissue of lies she'd invented for herself.'

She said slowly, 'She wrote me letters about you. Reams of them telling me how wonderful you were—and how much in love she was. She was so pretty, yet she'd never really had any serious relationships before, so I was glad for her. And, if I'm honest, relieved too.'

'Because she was going to be someone else's problem?'

'Yes.' Tarn winced. 'How awful that sounds. I'm so ashamed.'

'Don't be,' he said. 'It shows your instincts were working well. You should have listened to them and washed your hands of her long ago.'

'But I couldn't,' she said in a low voice. 'Her father was good to me. I always felt I had to look out for her, and Aunt Hazel too, for his sake.' She shook her head. 'I never knew how much Evie had resented that. Resented me.'

'Because you didn't know her.' He spoke forcefully, his eyes searching her face. 'Don't you understand, my love? You were guilty of nothing except being too loving and too loyal, and those are wonderful qualities, even when they're aimed at the wrong target.'

He sighed harshly. 'My God, I envied her for that, and wished with all my heart that I'd been the recipient instead.'

He paused. 'But I think what concerned me most was that you never actually asked me about this alleged affair. Faced me and demanded the truth.'

'Because I couldn't,' she cried passionately. 'Don't you see that? When I first met you all I could think about was avenging Evie's heartbreak. I told myself she was all that mattered. That knowing you'd been punished for your treatment of her might genuinely help her back on the road to recovery.

'Then when everything began to change and I fell in love with you, it was too late. Because you'd have wanted to know why I hadn't spoken before—why I'd been deceiving you about who I really was, and what could I say? I was trapped in all the secrets—all the lies, and going on seemed the only solution.'

She looked away. 'Besides, I was afraid what the truth might be. I could see how you might have become bored by her, and I was scared that you'd admit that you'd been using her after all. That you'd never given a damn about her but were making a fool out of a silly girl, simply because you could, and I—I couldn't bear that either. Because it might mean you could do the same to me. That you could break me and throw me away just as easily.'

Caz said almost helplessly, 'Oh, dear God.' He was silent for a moment, then: 'In all honesty, Tarn, I wouldn't have known what to say. I'd never taken stalking particularly seriously. Probably no-one does until it starts happening. Apart from saying "good morning" while she was working at Brandon, I don't think I said one word to Eve Griffiths. I certainly never saw her at the flat, and I'm not sure I even knew her name.

'Occasionally at social events, I was aware of being intensely scrutinised by a pretty blonde, but that's an occupational hazard for any bloke who's ever featured on a rich list.'

He shrugged, his mouth twisting ruefully. 'Some women come on to you, and you have to decide pretty early in life whether or not you'll allow that, and I decided against. I prefer to do my own chasing.

'In the end, it was only when the bad stuff started that the truth dawned on me, and for a while my life became hell on earth. At that time, I admit I would gladly have had her locked up and thrown the key away, so that part of your accusation was pretty much true.

'I thought once she'd agreed to have treatment, it would be over, but Jack Wainwright warned me it was never that simple, and he was right. At the moment, her attitude to me swings like a pendulum from one extreme to another, but Jack hopes that, over time, that will resolve itself.

'She's giving the police a bad time too, co-operating one day and in total denial the next.'

Tarn gasped. 'Is there nothing I can do?'

'Why, yes,' he said. 'You can leave her to the experts. Jack and his team can and will help her, once she accepts that it's her problem and no-one else's, but it will be a long haul and, as you found today, your intervention only makes matters worse. So you do not get involved.

'Besides,' he added. 'You're going to have other things on your mind, my sweet.'

'I—don't understand.' Her tone faltered a little. He hadn't moved a step but Tarn had the curious sensation she had only to stretch out her hand to touch him.

'Then I'll explain,' he said. 'I realised last night that nothing that had gone wrong between us actually mattered—not if the alternative was spending the rest of my life without you.'

'Caz.' Her words seemed to trip over themselves. 'Oh, Caz, you can't still want me—not after what I've done…'

'No?' He shook his head, the stark look fading from his face, to be replaced by a pleading tenderness that made her tremble. 'Then hear this. I meant every word of the note I left for you, Tarn. We may not have had the ceremony, but, by God, we had the wedding. You're still the only girl I'll ever love, ever need, and when you gave yourself to me, you became my wife, body and soul.

'There was no deception in that, Tarn.' His voice shook. 'It was love, pure and simple, and nothing can change that—unless, of course, you've decided that, because of all the other stuff, we're better apart.

'And even then I'm not letting you walk away, because we belong together and we both know it.'

He drew a breath. 'So, no more secrets, my dearest one. No more pretence. Just an old-fashioned marriage. A home together. A family. Is it a deal?'

She was never sure which of them moved first, only that they were in each other's arms, bodies pressed together in passionate intimacy, smiling mouths warm and seeking.

And when at last Caz raised his head, Tarn still clung to him, nuzzling his throat, breathing the scent of his skin, joy unfolding inside her like the petals of a flower.

He said unsteadily, 'Jack's been very tolerant, darling, but I think he might draw the line at us making love on his carpet. Where are you staying?'

'An airport place.'

He grimaced. 'It sounds as inviting as the place I picked. Why don't we collect your things, and find somewhere with four-poster beds and great food so we can begin our honeymoon.'

Tarn played with a button on his shirt. 'We're not actually married—if you remember.'

He kissed the tip of her nose. 'A minor point and strictly technical. After the honeymoon, we'll seek out a church with a friendly vicar, get him to call the banns and do the deed in style. I'll even get Jack to give you away.'

'Oh, God, I've got a hire car,' Tarn suddenly remembered as they walked hand in hand to the door. 'I'll have to return it.'

Caz shook his head. 'I'll arrange for it to be picked up,' he told her firmly. 'Because, my darling, I don't plan to let you out of my sight for some considerable time—day or night.'

Tarn laughed as she reached up, drawing his head down to her. 'That's definitely a deal,' she said, a world of promise in her voice. And kissed him.

* * * * *

Mills & Boon® Large Print
January 2013

UNLOCKING HER INNOCENCE
Lynne Graham

SANTIAGO'S COMMAND
Kim Lawrence

HIS REPUTATION PRECEDES HIM
Carole Mortimer

THE PRICE OF RETRIBUTION
Sara Craven

THE VALTIERI BABY
Caroline Anderson

SLOW DANCE WITH THE SHERIFF
Nikki Logan

BELLA'S IMPOSSIBLE BOSS
Michelle Douglas

THE TYCOON'S SECRET DAUGHTER
Susan Meier

JUST ONE LAST NIGHT
Helen Brooks

THE GREEK'S ACQUISITION
Chantelle Shaw

THE HUSBAND SHE NEVER KNEW
Kate Hewitt

Mills & Boon® Large Print
February 2013

BANISHED TO THE HAREM
Carol Marinelli

NOT JUST THE GREEK'S WIFE
Lucy Monroe

A DELICIOUS DECEPTION
Elizabeth Power

PAINTED THE OTHER WOMAN
Julia James

TAMING THE BROODING CATTLEMAN
Marion Lennox

THE RANCHER'S UNEXPECTED FAMILY
Myrna Mackenzie

NANNY FOR THE MILLIONAIRE'S TWINS
Susan Meier

TRUTH-OR-DATE.COM
Nina Harrington

A GAME OF VOWS
Maisey Yates

A DEVIL IN DISGUISE
Caitlin Crews

REVELATIONS OF THE NIGHT BEFORE
Lynn Raye Harris